Autumn Leaves Are Falling
A Spirit Town Cosy Mystery
Sarah Lewin 2024

This book is dedicated to:
Authors who inspire a sense of mischief, magic, and mystery
My teachers, parents, and author friends
My four beautiful grown-up children and my amazingly patient husband
I couldn't have written this without you

Chapter 1

Cemeteries don't normally freak me out. I surveyed the mess as I opened the door of my car. Walking through the gates my heart rose like a lump in my throat. Headstones lay cracked and broken, knocked out of their positions. By what? A car? No, too big. A motorbike? Was this random, an act of vandals, or something more malicious? Why would anyone knock over headstones in the old cemetery?

My blood thumped in my ears. Hot anger rose in my chest at the pointlessness of the destruction.

I re-read the text from an unknown number.

Check out the cemetery.

As owner of the local newspaper, I sometimes received anonymous tips for potential stories. Most leads came from people who were more than happy to leave their details. They loved to talk about what they consider newsworthy and important. They loved talking about themselves.

Whoever left this little breadcrumb for me to follow wasn't keen on sharing details.

I rummaged through my bag. Thankfully my water bottle wasn't empty. As I gulped the contents down, it soothed the dry burning sensation in my throat. Some days my emotional wellbeing tricked my body into feeling older than my years. My long dark brown hair was peppered with light grey. My mother and grandmother were grey by thirty-eight, the age I would turn in a few weeks. Dad called it highly strung, the anxiety and intuition that ran through the maternal side of our family. I refused to be tested or labelled, preferring to take each day as an opportunity to make a difference and to improve upon the previous days' efforts. If I had been labelled OCD, or ADHD or even anxious or depressed, it would be all too easy to curl up in a ball and read stories. Instead, I chose to report on them.

With my fists tightly clenched into a ball mirroring the tightness in my heart, I walked over to the plot where my parents and grandparents lay. Their final resting place was untouched, their headstones stood tall and undamaged. The destruction seemed random. That's only because I had not yet figured out the pattern.

I let myself breathe again. Taking a long breath in through my mouth and exhaling through my nose. In hindsight, the coffee and chocolate muffin I'd eaten an hour before could have been the cause of my current stomach upset and heart palpitations – too much sugar. Deciding to be constructive while I waited for the police to arrive, I took photographs of the damage.

It was five o'clock. I groaned. It was unlikely I'd make this afternoon's meeting. I was a volunteer on the committee, but I didn't like letting people down. Not that I expected it would take long for the new, and only, local officer to arrive from the station.

I heard the car before I saw the police sedan enter the cemetery. It pulled up alongside my little blue hatchback. Tall and slim, the policeman uncurled himself as he exited his car. This was our first meeting. My only contact so far had been by telephone; our last sergeant suddenly took early retirement a week or two ago. The paper reported family reasons for his abrupt departure. I had my doubts, but I had my parents' ethics and morals, and I didn't pay any attention to local gossip.

"Sorry I took so long." He offered me his hand. "Jon." I noted his casual clothes—black jeans, and a blue shirt with no tie, and wondered what his predecessor would have made of that. Jon's head was shaved. I guessed he was a red head, with his pale skin and freckles, blue deep eyes, and gingery eyebrows. Maybe a few years younger than me, he reminded me of the village bobby in a television show my mother used to watch.

I shook his hand. "Beth. Welcome to Spirit Town. As I said on the phone, I inherited the local newspaper from my parents. This is the text I received." I handed him my phone. "I've no idea who sent it, or why anyone would do this. I've taken some photos while I was waiting. I can send them to you if that helps."

Jon wrote in his notebook, before handing me back my mobile. "That would be useful. I'm still getting used to being the only police person in the village. I can call on the team from our neighbouring town if I need to. I'm sure I'll have to at some point, preferably just not in my first week."

"Do you need me to stay?" I asked. "I have a meeting I'm supposed to be at."

"All good. If I need anything else, I'll let you know. I don't suppose I can ask you not to report this yet?"

"Our next edition doesn't go to print before Friday. At this stage it will just be a couple of sentences in the local news section. I'll check with you before I finalise the edition to see if you have any additional information." I hesitated, before hopping back into my car. I felt bad, leaving Jon to work out this mess by himself. Should I be helping tidy up? It seemed disrespectful to leave the cemetery like this. "What happens next? Do you have to wait for forensics to take tyre prints? Does council come and repair the damage?"

Jon shrugged. "Nothing that fancy I'm afraid. I take more photos and try to match the tyre tracks with the type of vehicle, although realistically that's unlikely. Then I'll call our mayor. Someone will come out, assess the damage, cordon off the area for safety reasons and make the repairs. I have some police tape and witches' hats in the back of the car. I'll pop them around the most badly affected areas. We don't want people hurting themselves when they pay their respects to loved ones."

I peered at my watch. It seems pointless to rush to a meeting that may be over before I arrive.

"Let me send a text with my apologies and I'll stay and help, if that's okay?" I offered.

"I'd love the help, if you have the time," Jon admitted.

Held up at work, sending apologies, will catch up on any news early am tomorrow. I sent the text to Juliet, our local council marketing and events person.

"Have you heard of our town's annual Spirit Festival?" I asked.

"I've seen some of the flyers, but I haven't had time to read them." Jon pointed to the broken headstones near the gum trees along the fence line. "If you start on the left, I'll start the other side. Photos of the damage would be good. Also, of the ground—any signs of tyres, or anything that might identify something," he replied.

"Okay will do." We documented the scene via digital photos, hoping to find evidence lurking amongst the rubble. I decided to provide a little history about our festival. "Spirit Town doesn't have a local tourist attraction, like some towns have. We do have the Spirit Festival, every autumn. It's the prettiest time of the year, as the winds whistle through town blowing autumn leaves all over the place."

"What exactly does *spirit* mean?" Jon asked. "Or is that a silly question?"

"It's not a silly question at all. Spirit Town and Spirit Festival. The earliest record of the town talks about the tenacity of the people who braved the elements to cross the mountain range and settle here. They left the relative comfort of city life in Sydney. That pioneering spirit. Not giving up. Making a life on the land. Starting from scratch." I paused, remembering the story we were taught at school. "Years ago, the explorers who discovered the area settled because of its unique arable farming land. Nestled between the mountains and the river, whatever was planted, flourished. The earliest record of people settled here included a family who distilled the purest, finest whisky ever tasted in this newfound land. it was known as the town where the best spirit was brewed, hence the name Spirit Town." I stopped, noticing a few cigarette ends at the base of one of the tall eucalypts on the edge of the row of headstones. I took some photos; it might be an important clue.

"What did you find?" Jon joined me at the base of the tree.

"Probably nothing. I mean anyone could have been here, visiting relatives. Do you want to test one for DNA or is that just what we see on television?" I laughed, embarrassed at my question.

"I'll mark them as possible evidence. Who knows? Maybe they will be the clue that solves the case." He grinned. "So, what happens during the Spirit Festival?"

"It's a little different each year. Back in the early eighties, the fire spirit celebration was particularly popular. The wind spirit was not so well received. The devastating bushfires that swept through the outskirts of the town during that festival scarred the land for years. Farmers still talk about the fires of ninety-five. We have celebrated the land, water, the weather, ghosts, all sorts of things. This year we are celebrating the witch. The committee thought that would be fun, considering that magic and witchcraft is trending since the worldwide pandemic. Lots of tourists will pay to see a town dressed up like Halloween. We have a street parade, a float-your-boat on the river competition, an art exhibition, a dance evening, and everyone is encouraged to dress up."

"That sounds interesting. I think we have enough photos. All I need to do now is cordon off the area." Jon was already at the back of the sedan. He held up some police tape.

Once the sun disappeared behind the horizon the temperature dropped a couple of degrees. The eerie light and shadows added to the ambience in the graveyard.

"I volunteer on the committee for the festival. My mum and grandma used to volunteer so I kind of inherited the role. I don't mind, the festival is a bit of fun. It gets residents a chance to dress up, enter competitions, meet up with friends and forget their worries for a weekend. It brings tourists into the village for the weekend, so our small businesses are happy about that." What I didn't share with Jon, was that some of our residents got carried away with the theme, strange things tended to happen. Never like this though. The damage to the gravestones.

What worried me was why the guardians of the cemetery didn't stop the destruction. How could I explain guard elves to the new cop? Maybe that story was only a fairy tale to scare children from visiting the graveyard? I made a note to follow up whether our cemetery normally had any kind of security guards patrolling.

"Four cones aren't enough to keep people away. Council should be able to fix that tomorrow, hopefully," Jon commented as the light continued to fade.

"The police tape should add any extra layer of caution for anyone visiting," I reasoned. "I mean, I wouldn't barge through it."

"Thanks for your help, Beth. If you can send the photos through to my mobile that'd be great. I'll probably be talking to you in the next couple of days. I hope all goes well for the festival." Jon handed me a business card.

"I'm sure it will. Thanks."

As I hopped into my car the all too familiar pulsing in my head thumped, signalling the start of a migraine. Feeling under the front seat, I located the other water bottle which had rolled off the seat when I dumped my laptop bag earlier in the afternoon. Draining the liquid from the bottle eased the pain a little.

Stress migraines. Our local doctor told me many years ago. The doctor in the city had confirmed the diagnosis.

Mum told me the cause was my second sight—the intuition that follows the single female born in each generation. The doctors, who didn't know about my gift, blamed generalised anxiety. In other words, I worried too much.

I recalled Grandma's advice; to recognise my emotions by the energy flow in my body. I could feel it now, pulsing through my body. Nervous energy. A sign that I wanted to help ensure the festival was a success. My ties to this town were growing stronger each day.

I hadn't been entirely honest with Jon. When our town settled, many of the inhabitants sought to escape Sydney and live in peace and quiet. Those gifted with unique abilities, who were taunted for being different, felt safe here. My grandmother's journal mentioned an enchantment that surrounded the town. Invisible but effective. If Jon wasn't already aware of the specialness of the locals, he soon would be. *It's not up to me to tell him*, I reminded myself.

As Jon switched on his internal car light, a shadow darted behind the tree where I found the cigarette butts. *A trick of the light.*

The pain in my stomach reminded me that I last ate about eleven that morning, not counting the chocolate muffin. I drove towards the supermarket, looking forward to a big serve of salad—if there were any ready to serve packets left on the shelves.

The car park was nearly empty, which was only slightly unusual at six thirty on a Monday night. Maybe everyone else was more organised than me and went grocery shopping on the weekend.

Meeting okay. Only one issue. Coffee tomorrow 7am? I read Juliet's text.

My fingers tapped the screen. *Good idea. See you then.* I assumed we were meeting at *Evie's Cafe*, an unofficial meeting place for many locals. I was curious about the issue, but it could wait until tomorrow.

"Great minds think alike." I recognised Seamus's voice behind me as I stood unable to decide which bag of salad to take home.

Seamus and I had been friends most of our lives. He was only a little taller than me and he still had all his dark curly hair. Baldness didn't run in his family. His eyes were always smiling. We were inseparable growing up and people who didn't know our families thought we were siblings. We were always at each other's houses. When I returned to Spirit Town to bury my parents, it was as if we had spent no time apart.

"We missed you at the meeting tonight." Seamus only joined the festival committee because I suggested it.

"Sorry, unavoidable. Did I miss anything? Juliet said there was one issue, she'll update me in the morning."

"The usual. The oldies talking about how it all happened back in their day. Juliet did a great job diverting the conversation back to the present. She did carry on about how our mayor wants us to collect all the money from stallholders and the performers before the event. We can even pre book tickets." Seamus rolled his eyes, as he grabbed the last packet of Asian noodle salad.

"I imagine that revelation stirred up conversation." The more experienced committee members were old school. Pay cash at the door and boycott technology. I eyed the remaining salad choices, which are all unappealing. Seamus had grabbed our favourite.

"If you grab dessert, I'll share my salad. I ate a burger before the meeting, so I'm not starving." He teased. "You're right, there was lots of animated discussion. I tend to agree with the oldies on this. People don't want to commit to attending. They want to see what the weather's like or if they have other things to do, rather than feel they have to attend because they booked tickets."

"True. How about apple crumble? I think I have cream in the fridge if we're eating at my place." Dessert with apple sounded healthier than chocolate.

"Do you have leftover ice cream too?"

"Maybe." I tried to remember the contents of my freezer. My eyes ached and the effort of concentration made me dizzy.

Seamus arrived at the checkout, with a tub of ice cream, a few seconds after I did. "In case there's none in your freezer." He grinned. I put my finger to my lips. My ears pricked at the word *cemetery* from the group in front of us. I was thankful that Seamus trusted my instincts and didn't ask any questions.

"I heard that all the headstones were torn from their graves. The police don't know what sort of creature could have done that ..." Two youths were trying their best to impress the young lass serving them.

"You two want to be careful who you go around telling that story to. I'm sure the police will be interested to hear what you know about it. It sounds like a crime to me. Will I ring the station now and you can tell them what you know?" I said in what I hoped was a scary enough adult voice to make them think twice about embellishing their tale. Not that I thought for a minute that these two could have created that mess. Maybe they knew who did?

They looked Seamus and I up and down, as if deciding how to play their next move. "Er, we only heard it from a friend," the blond, pimply teen said.

"Yeah, not even a friend, just, you know, someone at school," the other mumbled as they picked up their bottle of fizz and packet of chips and disappeared out the door.

"If there's anything wrong at the cemetery, I'm sure the police will sort it out." I reassured the cashier as she scanned our items. I recognised her green eyes, freckles, and golden hair as one of the Wilson family. I remembered what it was like at that age, to have people try and scare you into using magic. The Wilson's were well known for being shape shifters. Hopefully she knew enough to stop from turning into an animal or a bird while she was serving customers.

"There she is." Seamus laughed as we walked to his car. In a nearly empty car park, Seamus had chosen the spot right beside mine. "The old Beth is back."

I knew he was referring to the way I had spoken to the teens. "I admit, it has taken longer than I thought to get my mojo back. Can you believe Mum and Dad have been gone nearly two years? I keep kidding myself that I'll sell up and move back to the city. I think when I joined the festival committee, I knew that I really wanted to stay. It feels like home again, most of the time. I want to make them proud. It makes it easier that I love my job—"

"Of course you do. You're the boss!" Seamus interrupted, waving the ice cream in the air. "I'm starving, and this will melt soon. I bet my old ute will beat your little car to your place!"

Seeing as Seamus was already in his car, I didn't doubt his claim.

With an uncanny knack of being right, Seamus had hit the nail on the head. I could finally admit it to myself. *I'm going to stay*. Decision made. I pulled my cardigan tightly around my shoulders as I turned the key in the ignition. The wind blew a little colder than normal, even for this time of year. I shook myself as an icy shiver wove its way up my spine. The spirit whispers around me remind me of my unfinished business. No wonder my migraine returned.

I just hoped it wasn't too late to make amends.

Chapter 2

The clock beside the pile of books on my bedside table confirmed my innate alarm radar was on track, waking me at my usual time of four thirty in the morning. It took me a few seconds to realise the throbbing in my temples had subsided. I took a gulp from the glass of water on the bedside table in case the migraine was simply dehydration, and not my second sight kicking in.

The water from my morning shower running down my back eased the remaining tension from yesterday's trip to the cemetery. I was sure that Jon and the council would be able to sort it out. Not my problem. Just because I had decided to stay for good didn't mean I had to start sticking my nose into everything. Let the experts do their job.

As I didn't have to meet Juliet until seven, I decided to turn on the radio. A quick peek in the fridge as I reached for the milk confirmed enough leftover salad for lunch. *Bonus.*

I dropped the tea bag into my cup, splashing drops of water on the counter. What did the radio announcer just say?

In breaking news this morning, we are reporting live from Spirit Town, where it appears someone has stolen the iconic gates that herald the entry way into the town for its annual Spirit Festival.

I didn't hear the rest of the news. My brain struggled to make sense of the words. Maybe I misheard the announcer, because what I thought I heard makes no sense. How could huge, heavy metal gates that would take hours to move get stolen overnight? Maybe they weren't missing. Had they been taken away to be spruced up before the festival? A long time ago, the gates were temporary; made of wood, they were only erected in the month leading up to the festival. The Macdonald family, their ancestors one of the founders of the town, donated a set of ancient gates, from one of their castles in Scotland, as a permanent fixture to the town's entrance.

I slid my lunchbox into the fridge, suspecting I might not get a chance to eat lunch today after all.

Cafe? Seamus' text was short and to the point.

Good idea.

Down the sink went what was left of my morning tea. Rinsing my cup, I left it in the sink next to last night's dishes. I sighed. My inner clean freak was fighting with my quest for knowledge. I wasn't sure who was winning.

Should I walk to the café? Better not in case I needed to get to the edge of town where the gates were located. Maybe a walk at lunchtime, depending on what the day brought. Climbing into my car, I was tempted to head straight to the gates—or rather where they should be, but Seamus had probably ordered our coffees already.

At just after six in the morning, a crowd of about twenty gathered at the cafe in the centre of town. Cars drove slowly past, looking for what—the missing gates? I saw the sparks of energy as some of our gifted residents sent out finder spells, trying to locate the gates.

"The gates form our identity; they are an important part of our culture." Our mayor's voice was unmistakeable. I walked up to where Seamus was waiting with two coffees in a cardboard tray. Max, our mayor, with a heightened sense of self-importance, puffed out his chest as he spoke to the reporter from the local television station. Bald as a badger, his suit jacket buttons strained over his belly. "We are the town with spirit. Our gates are replicas of medieval castle gates. Created over fifty years ago by Andy Macdonald. His family continue to be caretakers for the gates to this day."

"At least he is giving credit to the Macdonald family, even if he doesn't have the story quite right." Seamus said. "I spent some time with Andy, years ago. I've an idea of the amount of time and effort that goes into maintaining those gates. Did you know the family commissioned a ship and a crew to bring the gates out from the old country?"

Juliet lifted her right hand, motioning that she saw us. She disengaged herself from the group of old timers who were talking to her and headed toward us. Her long, blonde hair was tied into a bun fastened with bobby pins. I admired her cream suit. The mint green shirt underneath matched her bag and shoes. She was flustered; her brown eyes gave it away, glancing nervously around at the growing crowd of curious bystanders My gift of second sight allowed me a glimpse into the feelings of others, which was useful in many situations.

"I'll get you a coffee." Seamus senses people moods and feelings, though he doesn't always show it. He disappeared into the crowd, leaving Juliet and I alone.

"I want to talk to you about last night," Juliet said quietly.

"Seamus told me about collecting the monies before the event and pre-booking," I replied. "The concepts seem to make good business sense. I'm not sure how many people will pre-book. It's a good option for those who want to."

"Max was clear that we're to collect as much money as possible before the event. We can always refund if the weather prevents the festival going ahead, heaven forbid. Not a conversation I would be looking forward to." She rolled her eyes, with a pointed look in the direction of the mayor, still talking to the cameraman, who was slowly edging away towards the group of people gathered outside the cafe. "There's something else." Juliet looked around, agitated. Her nervous energy was almost visible, at least to me. I followed her gaze. No one was paying us any attention. "We've received a handful of notes threatening the festival. *If it goes ahead there will be trouble. Cancel. Don't proceed.* Vague and unclear comments. The writing was very childlike. I'm ninety percent sure it's just a prank. Max tore them up and threw them away." Juliet's voice was little louder than a whisper. I took a step closer, so I didn't miss what she was saying. "The good news is, Glenda was at the meeting. We have the full support of the gifted community. They are looking forward to this year's festival."

"That makes sense. The festival brings us all together. Gifted or not, we all love dressing up, entering competitions, eating different food from the food stalls, playing the carnival games. I'm going to put some witchy Halloween decoration's out at home. I overheard some kids in the street talk about the witch's house, at the top of the hill." I shrugged. "Kids have always called it a witch's house. Grandma loved it, though Mum and Dad weren't so keen. They tried to make it look more respectable, keeping the gardens neat and tidy. With the overgrown garden and dark paint, it won't take much to make it look the part." I paused as Seamus returned. Not that I meant to neglect the garden, I just never got around to it. The house was single storey, but with steps leading from the footpath up to the verandah. Grandma had created a witchy cottage feel.

"You would make the perfect scary witch!" He laughed, his hands full, holding a couple of bags. "Evie's parents have made free burgers. Want one?" without waiting for an answer he handed me a burger. "Much better than salad," he quipped, aware of my fondness for fresh fruit and vegetables.

"I'm going to find the mayor." Juliet said, heading off in the direction of the camera crew. I counted at least fifty people milling around outside the cafe now. I recognised a lot of them—residents, shop owners, committee members, well-known families, and farmers. Everyone must have heard the morning news.

"Evie normally manages the café by herself. Are her parents helping in the kitchen this morning?" I asked. Seamus pays so much more attention to detail about people's lives than I do.

"You're a journalist. How do you not know this stuff? I suppose you think finding information and investigating is different from gossip." He dodged as I made a fist aimed at his arm. "Bert and Bessie still prepare some of the food during the busy times. They are helping this morning because, well, look at the amount of people." Seamus gulped down his burger, eyeing the half-finished burger in my hand.

"Evie's parents look like they're loving the opportunity to catch up with their customers, their friends." I paused. "You may as well finish mine." I handed him the rest of my burger, still wrapped in the paper. I'm not really a breakfast person.

"Have you met our new policeman?" Seamus pointed to where Jon was talking to Lara, the owner of the local health food shop. A relative newcomer to the town, Lara had opened her store less than a year ago.

"Yes. Last night at the cemetery. I found the damage and called the station. He seems nice enough. It's a shame his first week in the town is proving so eventful though." I kept forgetting to check out the health food shop. It was on my list of things to do. "I'm glad the locals have decided to give the healthy options a chance. I saw some of the oldies in there the other day talking to Lara."

"Lara has a way of coaxing even the most sceptical customers to try healthier options," he agreed. There was something about the way he spoke. I wondered if he was becoming fond of Lara. She was a few years younger than me; and I was approaching forty. Her glorious honey blonde hair was tied back in a bun, little wispy curls escaping here and there. The few times I had spoken to her, I got the feeling we could become friends.

"I don't suppose anyone here knows anything about the missing gates?" Jon sighed as he and Lara joined us.

"I swear, normally we are a crime free town. I mean, apart from the occasional shoplifting or vandalism. Did anyone notice anything unusual?" I asked.

"No one saw anything," he said, his voice flat. "Many people had opinions on what to do with the offenders when we find them. Something about being made to wear high vis overalls and sweep the streets, weed the park, or clean shop windows."

"Yeah, we used to name and shame culprits. Less likely to re-offend that way," Seamus explained. "When there was a higher police presence. We were reclassified from a small town to a village when our population dropped to under two thousand. Police resources were reallocated to the bigger towns."

Facing the crowd, Jon raised his voice, and repeated his question. Only a few people bothered to respond, shaking their heads, mumbling, "Nope ... No ... Not me."

Jon persisted. "Well, if anyone does see the gates or hears anything about where they are, or what happened to them, please report it at the station. If you see anything else that's odd or unusual, please let me know." A few hands shot out for Jon's contact details. Most of the crowd started to wander off to get ready for work or school.

"My boss rang early this morning," Jon told us. "I'm to be provided with reinforcements, who will no doubt get in the way. It will be handy to have a second set of eyes and hands. I'd love to solve this before it gets out of hand."

"You look like you need some breakfast." Bessie handed Jon a freshly baked banana chocolate chip muffin and a cup of steaming hot coffee.

"Thanks." Jon smiled appreciatively.

Seamus's eyes followed Bessie as she passed out more goodies to those who remained chatting on the footpath. "You couldn't possibly be hungry!" I raised my eyebrows in mock horror. Seamus could eat more than anyone else I'd met. His high metabolism and nervous energy meant that he never put on weight.

Seamus chose to ignore my remark. "The mystery and the added tourist traffic will be good for business. It's the gossip and the whodunnit rubbish we need to squash. It's a shame there isn't a plausible explanation. Are we sure the gates weren't taken away to be repainted, or were damaged by a truck and had to be repaired?"

"Let's hope by Thursday we have some news. Maybe this is a prank for publicity for the festival. I'd love to be able to report in Friday's edition that the mystery is solved. Do you have any updates about the cemetery?" I asked Jon.

"What happened at the cemetery?" Lara asked, eye wide like saucers.

"Vandals knocked over some headstones. Council workers will be out there today cleaning it up." Jon looked at me. "A dirt bike was the likely weapon. It will be impossible to work out who was responsible. I would think there are many dirt bikes around here."

"I'd suggest it took more than a dirt bike to make the gates disappear," Seamus stated.

"True." The town clock chimed eight times. "I'd better get to the office. I'll ask Lexi to phone the radio and television stations and ask them to play down the drama and mystery. We won't get the tourists, with bad publicity."

"Well done, Beth." Max's voice oozed condescendingly. I had been so focused on our conversation I hadn't noticed the mayor standing behind me.

The rivalry between Max and me was something I never fully understood. Max moved to Spirit Town after finishing his apprenticeship as a builder. His rotund frame, created by years of burgers and chips washed down with fizzy drinks for lunch, made physical labour difficult. He managed his construction company by bossing all his employees, until there was no one left to bully. When he nominated for mayor, no one else opted to run against him and he won the position. For five years, Max had bossed and bullied people in town. Except people like me, who stood up to him.

Ignoring Max, I spoke loudly enough for most of those gathered to hear, "Bert, Bessie, thank you and Evie so much for setting up early and serving us the cuppas, burgers, and muffins. We all appreciate you guys." I turn to Jon. "I'll touch base with you before I print anything about the incidents. Do you have more business cards you can pass out, for people to ring if they know anything about the gates?" I tried to ignore the thumping of my heart as adrenaline coursed through my veins. My magic system was warning me of something. Unfortunately, I had no time to figure out what it was trying to tell me. Maybe Max was standing too close, and my body was reacting.

While Jon walked over to the people who remained in the street and handed out his business cards, Juliet came and stood next to me. Max frowned at Juliet and glared at me. He reached into the pocket of his jacket and pulled out his mobile. He marched away without another word to us.

"Thank you for speaking up just then. I probably should have, but Max is intimidating. I can't keep working directly to him." Juliet voice was little more than a whisper.

"Oh Juliet, that would be a shame. I do understand though. I couldn't work with him, and certainly not for him. Now, is there anything else you need from me, to promote the festival? Considering this morning's events." Most of the crowd had dwindled away. Seamus, Lara, and Jon wandered back to where we stood, as Juliet responded to my question.

"As long as nothing else happens, we should be on track. I know there is a saying about any publicity being good publicity. I'd much prefer the positive kind." Juliet hopped from one foot to the other. "Please don't take this the wrong way. While I'm still working for him, we probably shouldn't be seen talking too much. I want to leave on my terms, and not get fired, or be given some stupid job like emptying bins." Her mouth tried to smile, but her eyes filled with tears. I reached out to touch her arm. She turned away and hurried over to her car.

"Max is a bully," I told the others by way of explanation. "Juliet's looking for another job. In the meantime, she's juggling the nightmare of working for him."

"If you're heading to the office, I'll walk with you." Seamus said. I raised my eyebrows. His store was in the opposite direction, near Lara's shop. Jon and Lara, busy talking to Evie's parents, waved as we walked away.

"Has your second sight returned properly? Do you know what's going on in town?" Seamus asked. We walked past the bank, the accountants, and the solicitors, none of which opened before nine. *The Spirit Town Times* office was at the end of the street.

"If I knew anything I would tell you," I reassured him. "I haven't listened to my intuition for a very long time. I am more than a little out of practice. How about you? Do you have any inkling who's causing the trouble?"

Seamus shook his head. "I'm going to ask around. There was an odd feeling in the crowd. Did you pick up on it?"

Seamus was well known and well-liked by many in our village. I wasn't as gregarious. I didn't mean to be aloof; I couldn't help it.

"I thought it was aimed at me. You know how I feel about some of the gifted people in our community."

"As long as you realise, you're one of the gifted. One of us." The hug that Seamus sprung next surprised me. We didn't normally show affection. At least we hadn't for a long time. "Just make peace with what happened and let's move on." Seamus disappeared around the corner before I could respond. Before I could work out whether to follow him or not, I noticed Lexi waving at me. Soul-searching and peace-making would have to wait until after work.

Chapter 3

Lexi opened the door with a smile. Her mousy brown hair was tied into a plaited bun high on top of her head and her brown eyes shone with youthful excitement. "Have I told you how pleased I'm that we work together now?" I asked her. She was my sole employee—reporter and photographer. There were freelancers who submitted local stories from time to time, but most of the hard work was down to Lexi.

"Aw, thanks boss. I'm so grateful you chose me. You saw past my age and lack of experience. I love meeting people, talking to them, hearing their stories." She handed me a copy of that day's edition. "I get the feeling Friday's copy will be popular. Our town is all over the local news—radio and television. You probably know that already. I want to take some photos at the cemetery and the gates, or at least where the gates were. I've been playing with words to give the story an air of mystery, rather than a crime."

"That's a brilliant concept. It's exactly what I was thinking about on the way here. I took some photos at the cemetery yesterday you can use too." Lexi's honesty and her friendliness won her the position. Her willingness to learn was another attribute I admire. "If you see anyone loitering about, work your charm, chat to them and see what they tell you." I paused, remembering the more urgent task we needed to get straight onto. "Before you go, can you contact the radio and television stations, assure them that the festival will still go ahead and that we'll keep them in the loop with any news?"

Lexi scribbled lots of notes for everything I said. I liked that. I sensed her concern. Talking to clients was different to talking to more experienced reporters. Izzie and Sharon, the journalists, at the radio and television stations, had many years' experience. We had all been at university together, but they hadn't yet met my assistant. "What if we sit together and talk to them? I'll put the speaker on my mobile. You take the lead and I chime in only if you need me?"

Lexi's face lit up. "I'll come into your office. I can still see the door in case we get any walk ins."

By ten am, Lexi and I had convinced our contacts at the local news outlets that there was no sinister crime wave in Spirit Town. Assuring them that everything was on track for a successful festival, we promised to keep them updated with any development.

"A cup of peppermint tea and some grapes." Lexi placed a cup and a small bowl on my desk. "I'm going to take the camera and go and take some shots of where the gates were, the cemetery and some other shots around town. I'll talk to anyone who wants to chat; someone may know something." Lexi's smile said it all. Talking to people energised her. Talking to people drained me most days. At least it had until I learnt how to protect my energy.

"A great idea." I smiled at Lexi. "I'm going to go for a walk. Stretch my legs and get a feel for what is going on around town. We can all be such terrible gossips." I grinned. Half the time I forgot to spend a few minutes placing my invisibility cloak around myself before venturing outside. I visualised its vibrant shimmering energy surrounding me, keeping me safe and hidden, protected from anything that would drain me.

As I placed the *back in ten minutes* sign on the door, I observed that customers were lined up out the door of the café. Unusual for a normally quiet Tuesday morning. The additional traffic indicated people's curiosity. Driving down the street, what did they expect to see? I did understand the interest in the mystery of the missing gates, especially so close to the timing of the festival. People probably thought it was a gimmick to attract more tourists.

I crossed the street, heading in the direction of the park. It was a hunch more than anything else. Once I had ignored my inner voice, which was telling me not to drive over the bridge in the dark. The wooden palings had washed away in a freak surge in the river—the rising water brought about by one of the town residents' spells gone wrong. It was the persistence of my inner voice that made me swerve at the last minute. Only then did I see the water where the bridge should have been.

Stepping into the park, I gasped, my stomach churning at the sight in front of me. The fairy lights which normally adorned the poplars, the oaks and the eucalypt trees were cut and strewn in pieces around the park. Freshly planted flower beds were destroyed. Geraniums, gerberas, marigolds, and calendulas were uprooted and tossed aside. Tire marks tracked across the grass, as if motor bikes had tried to do wheelies in the freshly watered lawns. The black pop-up sprinkler heads had been torn out of the ground. This was senseless vandalism.

"Did anyone see what happened?" I asked the others, who were staring in disbelief. Their faces mirrored the way I felt, horrified at the sight before their eyes. Heads shaking no, mumblings of no. Onlookers started snapping photos. I wanted to tell them to stop taking pictures. Not to share anything on social media. I knew it was too late when I saw a couple of people talking on their mobile phones.

The familiar pounding just behind my left eye. Not quite a migraine, yet. I realised there was no way to put a positive perspective on this incident. Absent gates may have a reasonable explanation. I couldn't think of any justification for damaged headstones or the mess in front of me. I sighed. Feeling someone move beside me, I turned to my left.

"I didn't mean to startle you," Jon said, staring at the broken plants and dirt strewn about in front of them. "Didn't someone say that Spirit Town was quiet? Not much crime?"

Following his gaze, my heart broke a little at all the flowers upended and deposited in piles on the grass and the footpath. "There just aren't any words. I don't know what to think. Have your reinforcements arrived?"

"They'll be here by lunchtime. Three of them. Which I thought was too many, but now?" He scratched his head, staring at the mess. "Do you have any idea who could have done this, or why? Where should I start looking?"

I shook my head. "Most of our community support the festival. I can't imagine anyone wanting to cause this kind of negative publicity." I turned away from the once beautiful garden beds. A few people walked across the road, pointing at the fairy lights lying broken on the ground.

"Please don't touch anything. This is officially a crime scene." Jon walked over to stop a couple of women who moved to pick up some of the geraniums.

I knew exactly how they felt. My fingers tingled with the itch to pick up the plants and return them to the rich garden soil. The women were only trying to help. The energy in my fingers was quickly spreading to other parts of my body. My feet burned. I wriggled my toes, hoping that this surge of electricity was an indication that I would start to get some answers soon. A couple of elves, dressed in brown and difficult to see unless you were staring right at them, were sifting through the mess. Most likely trying to save as many plants as they could, with their own unique elfin magic.

Should I tell Jon a little more about the special abilities of some of our residents? That when it worked properly, one of my gifts was the ability to *see* events, either before they happened, or somehow *know* answers without a logical explanation. That knowledge would be useful for the local policeman. Would he be open to the mysteries of our town? I wasn't in the habit of telling my story to people. In light of the current series of events, I had the feeling that my ability to sense things might come in handy. I wasn't sure if he noticed the elves, but I assumed he just didn't see them.

"I'm not sure how to tell you this, so I'm just going to come out and say it. Some of the residents of our town have what can be called supernatural abilities. Seeing the future, the ability to change the weather patterns, knowing how people are feeling, curing illnesses, astral travelling, seeing and talking to ghosts, shapeshifting, innate knowledge that has no logic behind it. Most of the time, those without these abilities and those gifted locals all get along well with no dramas." I paused, glancing sideways at Jon to gauge his reaction.

The policeman appeared to be processing this information. At least he didn't laugh, so I continued. "The first time I sensed something was back in grade five. Billy was being a bully, as usual. Suddenly my fingers and toes started tingling. I remember as clearly as if I was watching it happen. I saw Billy knock Sam off the top of the monkey bars. Then Billy knocked Sam off the monkey bars in real life. Sam ended up in hospital to get a cast on his broken elbow," I confided to Jon. "At first, I didn't tell anyone. I was scared that, somehow, I had pictured it and made it happen, which of course I know now is nonsense. There were a few similar incidents, where I saw something happen just before it did. Then I started seeing events that already occurred, as if they were happening again. I thought I was going mad." I shuddered at the memory.

"Luckily my grandmother knew what was happening and spoke to me. All the women in our family have second sight." I figured that was enough information to start with. Jon tilted his head slightly to one side, indicating he had a question. Probably more than one.

"It'd be too easy to assume your gift has told you who stole the gates and trashed the cemetery and the park?" Jon asked hopefully. "Then we could solve this now and everything could go back to normal."

"That'd be nice, but no." I paused as my phone starting buzzing. I smiled apologetically at Jon and pressed the green button to take the call. "Hello. Yes, that's right. How did you? ... Of course, that makes sense, thank you. I'll be there in ten." I tucked my phone in the pocket of my black slacks. I turned back to Jon.

"That was Max. Someone filmed this mess. Not when it happened. Afterwards." I glanced around at the twenty or so people still standing around, taking photos or talking on their mobiles. "They sent the video to the local radio, and television stations. Probably the newspaper as well. The mayor wants an emergency meeting. Now. You should expect to be summoned as well." Jon's phone rang as I was speaking. I took my phone back out and sent a text to Lexi, letting her know what happened and telling her to expect calls or messages about it.

Jon and I walked together, behind the piles of dirt towards the back of the council chambers. I pointed out the room we were headed to. "Max commissioned contractors to build the room behind the existing council chambers. When it was built, cynics in the town had loudly grumbled that it was probably his contractors that won the job. I don't disagree. Nothing was ever proven. The room is used by many of our local groups including the festival committee. Twenty people fit comfortably in the room. Wait 'til you see the big table commissioned by the mayor. The little kitchenette is always fully stocked."

We heard Max's voice as we arrived at the door.

Jon asked, "Does he always yell at people?"

"He does," I confirmed. "He expects it to make people do whatever he tells them to do, instead of questioning him."

"It works more often than it should," added Seamus as he joined us. Lara and Juliet followed a couple of seconds behind him. As we waited in silence to be let into the room, I wondered Max's motivation for this meeting. Why were we the chosen few?

I smiled at Lara. Although she had only been in Spirit Town a short while, Lara had proved invaluable on several committees. The main street and the park beautification plans had been an idea she had brought with her and quickly garnered the support of the council and the other shop owners. And the idea to hold a fancy dress dance evening as part of the upcoming festival. Her workshops teaching people how to use common items found at the supermarket to improve health and wellbeing were popular across all age groups. I wasn't sure whether she held any supernatural gift or whether she was just talented in the normal way.

In addition to owning the saddlery and the fishing tackle shop, Seamus owned several farms in the area and was friends with most of the people in the town. His family had been in Spirit Town almost as long as mine. They'd built a significant portfolio and Seamus was the sole heir. A fact he didn't share with many people. Seamus was in my class on the first day of big school. We shared the same classroom for the next twelve years. If Max wanted local support for whatever he had planned, Lara and Seamus could be instrumental in providing that link into the community.

Juliet was Max's council representative on most of the local committees. She was the council marketing and media spokesperson.

I watched as an older man walked over from his car, which was parked in the disabled parking spot close to the building. He held his walking stick tightly, looking straight ahead at where we were gathered. I felt the jarring pain of every step he took. His head was covered with tuffs of fluffy white hair. I recognised Mr Garfield, part-time lawyer, and accountant. As he drew closer, I noted the additional wrinkles and the thicker glass in his spectacles since the last time I'd seen him. I took his Advanced English class for three years during high school. Quiet, unassuming, he could capture a room of pimply teenagers with his version of Shakespeare. Our class acted a punk version of Hamlet, at the end of year concert. Did he have a special gift, other than the gift of words? I'd never been able to figure that out. Mr Garfield was not on the festival committee. He was well respected by most of the oldies in the town. If Max's strategy was to have him as a spokesman for the older generation, I would have probably done the same. I had to admit Max called an interesting mix of participants for this meeting.

On cue, Max opened the door to the meeting room. A man I didn't recognise scurried away, eyes staring at the ground in front of him. Probably embarrassed to find an audience for the bawling out Max had just given him. The man reminded me of a mouse, timid and scared, wringing his hands together, clutching a notebook to his chest. He grey suit looked odd, it sat uncomfortably on his skinny frame. Was that Max's personal assistant, Ewan? Lexi mentioned Ewan, a distant cousin of hers, who was working with the mayor.

When the mayor finally moved out of the doorway we entered in silence, Mr Garfield the only one who directly acknowledged Max.

"I'll get to the point." Max started speaking as soon as Jon shut the door behind him. "Someone is trying to ruin our festival. I don't know if it's a rival town, or someone in town who doesn't like tourists. Every year there are hiccups, but not like this." Max's voice was rising, not yet yelling, his unmistakeable overbearing tone leaving no doubt that we were being berated for circumstances beyond our control. "I won't stand for it! This must be stopped. Jon, what are you doing to resolve this issue?" he demanded, thumping his hand on the desk in front of him.

"Well sir, er, Max." Poor Jon. I wouldn't have thought he was normally a nervous person. I was angry that Max put Jon on the spot like that, but I held my tongue, for now. I might need to speak up soon enough. Jon must be feeling bad that the town was on the news and that his bosses were sending in reinforcements. All in the first week in his new job.

Jon found his voice. Strong and confident. "Three more officers will be here in an hour. We have the incident room set up at the police station. One of the priorities will be following up with the people who were at the park this morning, those who took footage, and check to see if they captured anything useful. I'll put a call out for any witnesses to the destruction at the park, the cemetery, and the disappearance of the gates. They are huge incidents. Someone in town must know something." Jon straightened his shoulders, staring Max in the eye as he gave his update.

Everyone nodded. Seamus patted Jon on the shoulder. "Ring Izzie at the radio station. She'll help get the message out far and wide. People listen to her station. She can ask for anyone who was at the park to contact you." Jon took out his notepad as Seamus spoke.

Max continued, ignoring the interruption to his tirade. "Garfield, I can rely on you, as always, to make sure everyone knows we are doing our best to resolve the issue. The festival will go ahead as planned. The incidents are nothing more than bored teenage vandals. We will get to the bottom of this." Max said to

Garfield. It wasn't a question, more like a command. I couldn't tell by the older man's face what his feelings were about being ordered around by the mayor.

"Of course, Max," was all he said.

"The rest of you. Do what you have to do to make sure everyone knows that everything is okay." In the closed room, Max's voice reverberated loudly, giving the impression he was barking orders at us. I held my tongue. My inner voice told me now was not the time to call out his behaviour.

Juliet stood up. "Of course, Max," she parroted the words spoken before. Neither Jon, Lara, Seamus, or I spoke.

"I want a report back at the end of the day!" Max yelled as I led the others out of the meeting room.

The four of us walked in silence back towards the park. I watched Mr Garfield hobble to his car and drive away. Juliet hurried past us, head down. Her words about being worried to be seen talking to me, echoed as she scurried away.

"This is ridiculous! Juliet is too scared to talk to me for fear of losing her job. Max barks orders at everyone! I'm going to do some research myself and I don't think I'm going share with Max. At least not straight away. Why don't we meet at Evie's later this afternoon if you want to chat about how we can help solve this? Jon, I'm not suggesting we step on your toes, it's more about community liaison."

"Any insight into the town and where to start is okay with me," Jon responded. "Is five too late? I'll be busy briefing the others for most of the afternoon."

"Five works well for me. I close the shop then and I'll come straight to the café," Lara agreed.

"I'm always up for food at the café!" Seamus said.

As we all went our separate ways, I felt the nervous energy. We were all wondering one thing. What would happen next?

Chapter 4

"The phone's been ringing all morning," Lexi said as I arrived back at the office with toasted sandwiches.

"I didn't know whether the grumbling of my stomach meant I was hungry or anxious. I decided a strong cup of coffee and some food was probably the best option." Missing lunch would make it easier for another migraine to take hold. I handed her a brown paper bag with her favourite toastie—cheese, chicken and avocado, and a strong cup of mocha.

"Thanks! I was starving but I didn't want to leave here in case I missed any calls. Most people are worried. Will the recent events impact the festival? They've seen the footage or heard what happened at the park and the cemetery. Then there's the mystery of the missing gates. I spoke to Izzie and Sharon at the television station. They are so nice, I don't know why I was worried earlier. We don't know a lot of information yet, and we don't want to encourage the rumours and gossip. So, we're going to focus on the positive aspects of the festival. What a great weekend it will be. *'Visit Spirit Town for a weekend escape from the normal daily grind.'* That sort of thing. Encourage entries into the competitions. I'll create some social media posts with the same message. More about how great the festival is going to be to create some positive chatter. Give people something else to talk about, to look forward to."

"I think that's just perfect. I was so caught up in what was happening I wasn't thinking big picture. That happens after a meeting with the mayor." I rolled my eyes. Lexi shared my opinion of Max. "You're coming up with some awesome ideas for our paper. I'm so glad you decided to apply for this job," I told her. "I'll be at my desk. I've an awful niggling feeling that I'm missing something important." I rubbed the back of my neck. It achedwhen I was stressed, or tired, or both.

"Your second sight still not working properly?" she asked, her brow furrowed with concern. Lexi knew I was intuitive and had premonitions sometimes. Her family, part of Spirit Town for generations, were not gifted with supernatural powers, but they were the most creative bunch; winning prizes at the local show most years. Despite being up against entrants who used a little extra 'zing' in their work.

"Nope. It's like I have a faulty switch that keeps turning off every time I try to concentrate on it."

"Then don't focus on it," Lexi said, as she opened the bag that contained her toastie.

Maybe she was right.

Surveying my desk, I moved my laptop to the right, and piled the loose papers strewn about my desk onto the shelf behind me. I was way behind on my filing, and I didn't like to ask Lexi to do my boring work. It was my responsibility.

Opening my toastie bag, I took a bite of the sandwich. Savouring the taste of melted cheese, tomato and avocado on multigrain. Evie's toasties were awesome. Her strong mochas were amazing, too.

Ten minutes later, the blank page on my laptop screen stared at me. The cursor blinked, waiting for my inspiration.

Nothing. Not a word or an image filled the space in my brain.

In desperation I grabbed a pen and opened my notebook. Sometimes the old-fashioned ways were the most effective.

Still nothing.

Frustrated, I closed my eyes, and slowed my breathing.

An image of an ogre picking up one of the town gates flashed up in front of me. I opened my eyes. This couldn't be my second sight. Spirit Town wasn't home to ogres, dragons or unicorns. Except in the bedtime stories to discourage children out after dark. We had a few resident elves and fairies that helped out some folk. Evie's Café for example, fairies helped out the back, making sure there were enough clean plates and mugs for customers. While it was not quite a typical country town or village in Australia, and was home for some folks with unusual skills and talents, we weren't hiding a family of ogres. Witches—probably. Other magic beings—possibly.

I closed my eyes again. Nothing.

My ability to see things that were going to happen had become hit and miss, stuck behind a veil I couldn't break through. Maybe because I hadn't practiced my gifts in ages? Or because I was the last of my clan? At thirty something my parents were married with a baby on the way. The knot in my stomach returned, reminding me of all the things I still wanted to achieve, and of all the mistakes of my past.

A tiny voice prompted me to *make amends and move on.*

I shook my head, clearing away the cobwebs and memories.

Later. There would be plenty of time for that after we solved the current problem. After the festival is over. The image of the ogre returned. Must be because I was tired, we didn't have ogres running lose through the town. The real answer had to be simpler than that.

THE WEATHER WAS UNSEASONABLY cool, even for autumn. Were some of the residents messing with our climate again? It happened frequently, making it difficult to tell the difference. Except for that time, we had snow in December, when someone felt like a white Christmas. The falling leaves spun around me as I returned to the park. I wanted to have another look at the damage. I watched as George, the council gardener, knelt on the edge of one of the garden beds, gently returning soil to the gaps where the plants used to sit. In his late fifties, he was one of the many people Dad had time for.

"None of the plants can be salvaged," George confirmed. "The good news is, I'll be replacing the plants first thing in the morning. I've the plants on hold at the nursery," George reported. I knew by the smile on his face that he was proud at being able to do his bit for the town. He donated much of his spare time, helping some of our elderly residents by tending to their gardens.

I was restless, filling in time until the meeting at five. What did I expect to see? Someone creeping around looking like a criminal? I wandered deeper into the park. A place I loved; I had been coming here for many years.

"Do you mind if I walk with you?" George ambled up behind me.

"I don't mind at all."

"I think you must love the park nearly as much me, Miss Beth," George said amiably, as we walked through the main 'top' park into the 'bottom' park. The downstairs park always reminded me of a rainforest. "Did you know that some of these older trees were planted over one hundred and fifty years ago, when the township was first settled? We have a mix of evergreens and deciduous trees. Some are natives and others were imported from Scotland." George was like a walking plant encyclopaedia.

We walked the path that wove through the sheltered glade of trees, cypress, oak, birch, maples, pines and elms. Leaves of all shades of green mixed with the rich reds and oranges and lighter yellow autumn leaves. Wooden benches sat at several spots, and picnic tables in other places. On weekends, families picnicked while the oldies came out from the neighbouring retirement village and sat reading their books.

From the sanctuary of the bottom park, the mess was invisible. I lingered a little longer, after George waved and crossed the road to the council depo. I didn't much like reminiscing about the past. Being in this beautiful space reminded me of a time when I was only young. Mum and Dad had brought me to the park for a picnic. Was it a special occasion, or a spur of the moment family outing? I felt the energy of anticipation and happiness captured in that moment. Another snapshot, as a teenager, hanging out with twins, Silvie and Tanya. Sharing a bottle of orange fizz and packets of chicken chips. Our club, the sisters of spirit as we called ourselves, met a few times, until their family moved away. Their father worked on the railroad, as an engineer. He job meant postings every five years. Around the time of our sixteenth birthdays. I was reluctant to move, to leave this special energy I felt, the connection and closeness to people from so long ago.

Knowing I had a meeting to attend, I took the three steps back up to the top park. At least the vandals had left the swings and slippery dip intact and undamaged. The park was a haven for people of all ages. It made me furious, that someone felt the need to vandalise the park, tear down the fairy lights and rip up the plants.

The day was nearly over, and the fading light made the park gloomy and maudlin, without the fairy lights to light the way. I wasn't the only person wandering in the park. Mysteries and crimes tended to bring out those with inquisitive, curious minds. I recognised a few as locals, or familiar faces from when I was growing up. There were a few faces that weren't familiar. "That's not a mystery," I muttered to myself. "Even I can't know everyone who lives here."

"Talking to yourself now, Beth," Seamus said, coming up beside me.

"Not at all. I knew you were there," I replied with a smile. "Do you think any of these people are guilty of this mess? Or are they just checking it out?"

"Probably just curious. I know we said this is probably the work of bored kids, but honestly, I think this is something different. Dark. At least, that's my sense of it." Seamus shrugged.

"I've been thinking the same. I get the feeling that I'm missing something. And before you say it's me needing to know the answer to everything, that's not what I mean," I said. "I have a sense that the answer is just out of reach. I can't put my finger on it and that annoys me."

"Your intuition is still on the fritz?" Seamus asked.

"Yes, it's so frustrating," I responded.

"I think you're trying too hard."

I thought about that for a few seconds. "While I don't like to admit it when you're right, I think it's one of those times. I had an image pop into my head earlier today; that an ogre had taken the gates. We don't have ogres here in Spirit Town."

Seamus scratched his head, "Did you say an ogre?"

I nodded. "Don't tell me you know where one lives." I couldn't help the sarcasm; recent events had upset me more than I was willing to admit.

"This might sound a little far-fetched, but there is a brand of truck called an Ogre. Farmers around here use them to transport heavy items. I wonder if your gift is working again after all. A farm truck like that's definitely big enough to transport the gates."

"Really? Seamus! That's genius! Let's tell Jon and the others." A shiver across my back confirming that we may be on the right track after all. Did we accidentally find a clue?

"Whoa, steady on. It was only a thought. Do you know how many farmers there are around here who might use an ogre? We can't go and search every farm."

"We can and will if we have to. It sounds like the best, and only lead we have. You can stay here if you want. I'm going to tell Jon."

"There are still a couple weeks before the festivities. If someone's trying to ruin the festival, why start now? They would be better off waiting until a few days before it starts," Lara mused. She and Jon had arrived at the café before us and were already talking about the events of the last twenty-four hours. Seamus and I slid in beside them.

Evie's Café was far more than just a place that served coffee. We were seated at one of ten pine booths. Matching red and white table clothes adorned each of the tables. At the other end of the space were two long bar tables for people to sit and use the free Wi-Fi while they ate. In one corner, the children sized furniture was popular. A mural on the wall depicted a range of fairytale characters and mythological creatures living on a farm with llamas, horses, and sheep. A wooden shelf contained some toys and books. Parents enjoyed their food seated at tables nearby. Children behaved, eating their meals with a sense of independence. An old-fashioned juke box in one of the other corners played a large variety of music from the last six decades.

"There's an impressive variety of food here." I followed Jon's gaze. The menu was written in large print on the blackboard that ran the length of the wall behind the counter. Depending on the day, options included sandwiches, pub style meals, pizzas, burgers and chips. Then there was the dessert menu.

"It's brilliant! I could eat here every day." Seamus grinned.

"How does Evie get time to cook all the food as well as serve? She must get up super early every day and stay back late," Lara commented.

"She does." I grinned at Seamus. He opened his mouth to say something, but closed it instead, returning my grin. "Her parents help. Bessie and Bert were here this morning handing out food and drink."

"It certainly seems a popular place." Jon was stating the obvious. Most of the tables were full, even on a Tuesday night. Families loved that *kids ate free* a couple of nights a week. Tonight's special was tacos.

"If it's someone who is trying to cause damage, to drive tourists away, they probably aren't thinking rationally," Jon offered, steering the conversation back to the current series of events. "You would be surprised how many people make stupid choices. They don't think things through."

"We have a hunch," Seamus said, sliding in the booth beside Lara. "Beth saw an ogre, which makes no sense. Except, that Ogre is a brand name for a truck that many of the local farmers use." Lara and Jon looked at each other, turning back to Seamus and me, eyebrows raised, a slightly puzzled look on each of their faces.

"My second sight hasn't been terribly reliable lately. I saw an ogre when I was thinking about the gates. Do you have any other leads?" I asked Jon.

Evie arrived at the table. "Are you guys ready to order?" she asked.

"Can we have a round of hot chocolates, and a large plate of your loaded fries, please?" Seamus asked. Evie nodded and smiled as she wrote in her notepad.

"Can we also have some cheesy bread?" Lara added. "If we're going to load up on carbs, let's do it properly." She winked.

Jon tapped the table as Evie walked through the swinging door that led to the kitchen. "Point of order. Less talking about food, more talking about this case, whatever it is. So, you were saying ogres? Trucks called ogres. We might as well start somewhere as sit around waiting for something to happen." He turned to Seamus. "Do you have any idea how many farmers locally have these trucks?"

"A lot. It isn't like I have a register of people who have farm trucks, ogres, or even a list of farmers, although that would be useful." Half teasing, half serious, Seamus continued, "Actually, I do have a list of sorts. I started a customer mailing list for the different promotions we've held over the years. We could start there."

Before anyone at the table could answer, old Mr Todd wobbled towards them, waving his walking stick in the air. His hunchback worse than last time I saw him, which would have been my parents' funeral. He turned to Jon. "You should be investigating the potatoes! It's all about the potatoes! Or was it the pumpkins, maybe it was the pumpkins! You're the detective, find them, before they ruin us!" He screamed. Seamus half stood up, turning towards old Mr Todd as he tripped. Raising his hand at Seamus with a frown that said *don't touch me* he righted himself and tottered off to his seat against the wall.

No one spoke. The café, still full of customers finishing their meals, fell silent. After a few seconds, as if a switch flipped, people started talking again as they hurriedly finished their meals. Most of the tables were empty within ten minutes of Mr Todd's revelation. Mr Todd left the café, shooting our table a frown that I think was meant to scare us into some kind of action.

"Well, that was fun," Lara said. "This food though, is delicious. If I'm going to eat comfort food, it's Evie's food every time."

"Crazy old codger. He used to be our headmaster. Can you believe that?" Seamus told Lara and Jon.

"Mr Todd was, and probably still is, a very intelligent man. With several degrees he has achieved some amazing feats. He taught English in Africa and parts of Asia. The dementia started showing before he retired. He refuses to be put in a home, and still takes care of himself." Seeing the look of concern on Lara face, I clarified, "His son and daughter live on the property, too. His son farms onions, garlic, and leeks. His daughter is a teacher. There are three individual houses on the farm. It's been in the Todd family for years."

The noise my stomach made told me it was grateful that I was eating for the second time today. We were silent as we sipped our hot drinks and wolfed down the cheesy bread and loaded fries. Greasy takeaways sat like a lump in my stomach, but not the food from Evie's. Did she use gluten in her breads, or was there a secret magical ingredient that saved my stomach from feeling sick? I could savour the comfort food and not feel ill for days. Her hot drinks too, must have a level of magic, saving us all from the evils of normal dairy products.

"If we take Mr Todd at his word, are there any potato farmers in the area? Or pumpkin farmers?" Jon asked Seamus. "I mean, I do think the old guy is crazy but at this point I'll follow any lead we are given."

"Funnily enough, we only have one farmer nearby who farms potatoes and pumpkins. Back in the day there were more, now there's only the Neilson family. On the old Anderson place," Seamus responded. "They only moved in about a year ago. There was a story about them, something unusual. I can't remember what it was."

"Oh, I nearly forgot," Lara said, as she finished the last of her drink. "Juliet came into the shop to see me. I invited her to join us at the café. She thanked me but declined. Should we update Max on what we have pieced together?"

"No. At least I'm not going to." I looked at Jon, softening my voice a little. "If you feel you need to update him, that's fine."

"Let's wait until tomorrow and see what the day brings. I'm going back to the station. The others are sifting through the photos we took of the crime scenes." Jon opened his wallet and pulled out a twenty dollar note.

"My shout. You can pay next time." Seamus waved away his money.

I yawned. "I'm sorry, suddenly I feel really tired." My eyes were feeling heavy, and my arms were aching. My legs ached when I stood, as if I'd been working in the garden all day. Was I coming down with the flu? A dose of peppermint tea when I get home. One of my grandma's remedies.

"You two stay and have one of Evie's famous cheesecakes. We'll catch up tomorrow." I left quickly, so Seamus didn't feel obligated to make sure I was okay.

THE ACHE WAS WORSE at that point in the middle of my forehead. My third eye felt fuzzy sometimes. The worst thing to do was rub it. I learnt that years ago. Closing my other eyes helped. Sitting at the kitchen table, I contemplated my cup of tea.

I blinked as a light flashed outside the kitchen window. A second flash. Taking my mobile as a flashlight, I opened the back door. Reaching into the cool box on the verandah I picked up a couple of carrots.

Along with the house, I inherited Buddy the sheep. One of the benefits of having a sheep in the garden meant less mowing. Dad's fencing system made looking after Buddy even easier. I had to remember to feed him, and occasionally move him into a different area in the backyard. "Hey Buddy, I've a treat for you." The sheep met me at the bottom of the three steps. The warm fluff on his nose tickled as he nuzzled my hand offering a carrot. "Did you see anything unusual out here?" Buddy nudged the second carrot out of my fingers.

A few more minutes with Buddy revealed no more lights, or anything else unusual. The silence in the garden interrupted only by the occasional engine sound as a car drove past.

Plop!

A green frog landed at my feet.

Plop! Plop! Plop!

I turned, watching it jump along the wooden palings towards the back door.

An image of Grandma sitting at the little table on the verandah flashed in front of my eyes. *Forgive yourself.* Her words echoed.

I remembered the conversation as if it was yesterday. My last conversation before she passed. I licked the salty tears that ran silently down my cheeks.

Chapter 5

*M*eeting 8 am

The text message from Max wasn't a surprise. I dropped into the office to let Lexi know where I'd be.

Meeting Max. Back as soon as I can.

I scribbled on a post it note, leaving it next to the note she had left for me.

Following a lead. Back soon.

Max and Juliet had papers spread all over the table. "The other committee members send their apologies. I've assured them any decisions made here are in the best interests of the town." Max beckoned to me to sit down. Seamus, Jon and Lara were sitting opposite Max. I chose a chair next to him. A trick mum taught me. I sensed him squirm. A small movement, moving his hips and his shoulders—an attempt to assert his authority.

Juliet held up a flyer. "This time each year we take the publicity shots for the festival. Wednesday is scheduled as the day for taking publicity shots of the park and the gates. That's today. We need to make a decision. Do we go ahead with the festival, and the publicity shots? We could just use photographs from previous years."

"Or do we do something different?" Lara suggested. "Just because we've always taken photos of the park and the gates, doesn't mean we have to. We could shoot some videos. I'm thinking we could ask some of the oldies, the long-term Spirit Town residents what they think of the festival. Why it's important and what it means to them. It would make a great promotional advert for the festivities and the town itself. Beth, do you have contacts at the local radio and television stations? Would they be willing to show the video? The radio could play the audio."

"That's a great way to promote our festival and celebrate the lives of some of our inhabitants." I looked directly at Max. "What do you think?" Years of working with people like Max, and watching how he behaved, meant I was pretty sure I knew how to coax him on board. The trick was to make him think the whole thing was his idea.

Picking up on my cue, Jon asked the mayor, "How would you like us to play this? We could cancel the festival, wait and see what happens, or get out in front and get some positivity back in our town. I have the extra resources to find the vandals. Seamus has offered to provide a brief history on some of the farms in the area, in case there is any truth to Mr Todd's outburst last night. Beth and Lara can work on getting the video campaign up and running." He paused for a couple of seconds. "You're the boss."

Max perked up. He stopped clicking his pen on the top of the table. "I am, aren't I? The boss I mean." He beamed, looking around the table. "I can beat these good for nothing, meddling, nosy, criminals! They'll be sorry they started carrying on in our town! Seamus, Jon, go and talk to those potato farmers, now. Beth, Lara, get a list of people who will look good and speak well in the videos. I want that list today. You tell them you're asking on behalf of the mayor; they'll have to say yes then." Max was on a roll. I tried to stop the corners of my mouth forming a smile. I looked across the table. The others were seemed to be having the same trouble. Seamus must have tried to kick me under the table because Max's body jerked like he had been stung by a bee.

"Come in," Max called as a timid knock sounded on the door of the meeting room.

"Sir, there has been another incident," Max's personal assistant, Ewan, stuttered, peering around the door. "In the main street. You'd better come and see. All of you." Exiting the room, we followed Ewan out the room, through the double doors out into the street. Max's assistant still reminded me of a timid little mouse. He was skinny, maybe early thirties, short blonde hair, and green eyes. He wore that same grey suit and it still looked too big.

It was close to nine in the morning on a Wednesday. The street should have been bustling with people going to work, running errands and coming back from dropping their kids to school. Instead, a large group of people were huddled around the footpath outside the entrance to the park.

I quickened my pace as a feeling of foreboding ran down my spine. So much for thinking my gift had returned. I hadn't foreseen any of the recent incidents. In the past, my second sight had proven reliable. I wondered briefly if the perpetrator was able to block my sight. The others arrived seconds after I did. It was easy to see what everyone was staring at. In bright red paint, emblazoned on the concrete were the words STOP THE FESTIVAL OR ELSE.

"Four incidents in three days. Someone is seriously trying their best to scare the community and stop us going ahead with the festival." Juliet whispered, looking up at Max for guidance. Our mayor was slowly backing away from the crowd.

Out came mobile phones as people started filming the mess or taking snap shots. It was eerily quiet, as if no one knew what to say. I was furious that someone was deliberately causing this anxiety and trying to force us as a community to cancel the festival. Max was a few feet away, his phone held up to his ear. I'd bet that there was no one on the other end of that mobile. I cleared my throat and spoke loudly so that the thirty or so people gathered would hear me.

"I know this may look serious, but the paint will wash off easily. I bet this's just bored teenagers, daring each other to pull these stunts. To see how much drama and gossip they can cause. No one really wants us to cancel the festival. The police will work out who the perpetrator is and deal with them. The gates will be back up where they belong before the festival. The garden at the park will be bigger and better than ever by the end of the day. If anyone knows anything, please go to the police station and have a chat with them. Otherwise, let's just go about our day as we normally would. Let's not pay any attention to any of this." I could feel Max, Jon, Seamus and Lara staring at me, along with everyone else. I stood my ground, smiling and nodding at the residents as they dispersed, until it was only the five of us left standing, surveying the graffiti.

"Do you really think whoever is doing this will stop if we don't pay them any attention?" Lara asked. "What is your intuition telling you?"

"Not sure at the moment. I'll get back to you on that." I replied.

"I trust you're going to follow through with those promises, Beth," Max said sternly He had joined us once the crowd had wandered away.

Seamus winked at me. "Are you angling for a role on council?"

"Do you know who is doing this?" Jon asked hopefully.

Looking around to make sure no one was lingering, I replied, "I've absolutely no idea who's doing this or why. It does feel a little like bored teenagers though, I didn't make that up. I admit I may have gotten a little carried away. I don't like not knowing what's going on. I'm cranky that someone's trying to ruin our festival. People are looking forward to having some fun. I wanted to reassure everyone that it's all going to be okay and to rattle the person who's creating the fuss. To goad them into slipping up and letting me see what's next."

Seamus nodded. "I understand that. It won't take long to clean this up. I can get Jake straight onto it. I'll mind the shop while he does that." He nodded at Jon. "After this is cleaned up, are you up for a trip out to the Nielson's farm?"

"Sounds good to me. I'm going to have two of the constables randomly patrol around town, while the third stays at the station to answer any calls or walk ins," Jon agreed.

"Lara and I'll work on the plan to video the residents talking about our Spirit Festival. Right after I give George the news that we are going to increase the size of the garden in the park. We can regroup at the café at midday." I noticed Lexi was standing outside the office. I made a mental note to talk to her as well.

"I'll leave you all to it then," Max blustered. "Like we said back in the room—you will get it all done, sort it all out. I'll be in my office doing mayor tasks. I won't be at the café. I do expect a brief by the end of the day."

"How can I help?" Lexi joined us, as Jon and Seamus left to sort out their visit to the Neilsons.

"Lara and I are planning to video some locals about what the Spirit Festival means to them. A good news story, promoting our festival and our town. Could you set up the video system in the meeting room? I must talk to George before I do anything else." I watched Max walk back to the council chambers with his phone up to his ear.

"I'll take a couple of photos here. Then I'll head back to the office. The video will be set up in the room, whenever you need it," Lexi said.

"I'll order us coffees at the café, after I check in at the shop," Lara suggested. She and Seamus employed a couple of the younger residents of our town, who completed school and weren't keen to move to the city, in their establishments.

"GEORGE WASN'T AT THE park, or the council depo." I joined Lara at the table by the door. I could hear random words, *paint, gates, cemetery, festival* from those in the queue. The recent events were proving good for business in the café. I resisted the urge to tell them to stop, and to talk about something positive instead.

"Do you have an idea of who we should interview for the video?" Lara asked as we waited for our coffees.

"I do. I've a list on my laptop." I clarified my statement, "We ran a story a few years ago, interviewing families who have lived here for over eighty years. I was thinking we could contact them, pitching it to them as a follow up to the original piece."

"That's a great idea. I've got Sally minding the shop today, so I'm all yours. What do you need me to do?" Lara asked. Sally used to work at one of the corner stores, but her quirky clothes and singsong voice was too much for some of the old-fashioned locals. When Sally was happy, everything she touched seemed to shine and sparkle. It was good to hear she was working for Lara.

"I'll talk to my contacts at the radio and television stations. We often work together on local stories. They'll probably run the story later this week for us." I opened my laptop and located the list of names and contact details. "Lexi is great with technology. She'll have the room set up by now. I invested in the mixed media tech when she joined the team. Her skills will come in handy with this project." My energy pulsed through my third eye. It was a weird sensation. I hoped it meant my second sight was kicking in. "I've just emailed you a copy of this list. Could you please ring each of the families? Let them know we are following up on the original story and we want to run the video and audio as part of an advertising campaign for the festival. I reckon they'll all jump at the chance to be involved." I paused as Evie handed us our coffees in takeaway cups. "Thanks Evie, we'll be back for lunch. I'm looking forward to some of your pumpkin soup."

"I'll save you some." Evie smiled as she dashed back to the counter to serve the growing line of people waiting to order.

"The email contains confidential information. Eight people, their addresses and phone numbers," I told Lara. "For your eyes only."

"Of course." Lara nodded. "When do we want them to come in?"

"Let's say this afternoon about 2 o'clock. We can film it as a group." I stood up, gathering up my laptop and my coffee. "See you back here around midday, or a little before." Lara stood up, picking up her coffee. We waved at Evie as we left the cafe.

LEXI WAS ON THE PHONE when I returned to the office. I went straight to my desk and opened my laptop to draft a rough plan for the afternoon. An informal chat. The locals all knew each other and loved talking about their families. They'd be on board to promote the festival.

Lexi came into my office. "The room's ready. I've tested all the equipment. Ten chairs are set up around the table. Tea, coffee, and an urn in one corner. You can pick up the muffins when you go to lunch." Lexi's words tumbled out, a sure sign she was excited about the video idea. "I was impressed by your speech this morning. Very photogenic, and brave."

Noticing the questioning look on my face, Lexi continued, "Someone filmed your pep talk at the park. It's all over Facebook, and probably other social media as well."

"Oh goodness, I didn't say anything extra ordinary. I'm a little surprised that anyone would bother to film me."

The phone at the counter interrupted whatever Lexi was about to say. I was grateful for the quiet time. My third eye tingled and a weird noise buzzed in my ears. I squeezed my eyes shut. The noise in my ears got louder, like someone tuned up a radio, creating static white noise. I opened my eyes. Lexi was still talking on the phone.

What would Grandma do? That was easy. She'd sit and all the answers would be whispered to her. I hadn't inherited her peacefulness. I was more like Mum. Busy, distracted. With a highly tuned sixth sense. I doubted my ability. Tried to hide it. To fit in. To be normal.

Then why I couldn't drag myself back to the big city? Could I be sick of hiding and finally ready to be myself? Normal here could mean many things.

Playing with the weather. Moving objects. Astral travelling. Predicting the future. The buzzing lessened. The tension pulling across my forehead slackened.

If I stopped living in the past and forgave myself, would that be so bad? I closed my eyes again. This time an image formed. A group of people. Not a clear image, but a sense that the younger ones in the group were being told to cause the damage. No matter how much I focused on the image, the answer eluded me. Unable to gain any additional insight, I opened my eyes.

Lexi was standing in front of me with a grin on her face. "Meditating or asleep?" she teased. "Five callers now, all commending your motivational speech this morning. A couple of people offered to clean the paint if we needed help. The community spirit in this town is amazing. Why don't you go for a walk before your meeting at the café? I have everything under control here."

WALKING IN THE OPPOSITE direction to the area that was damaged, everything felt different. As if I could feel the trees and the plants. *Whisperings of spirit*, my grandma called the ability to tune into the elements. It was news to me, that I could tune into the spirit of the air, the earth, nature; it was a little disturbing. Maybe I would get used to it. I shivered, walking a little faster. I sensed eyes watching me. The hairs on my arm rose, sending the shiver throughout my body. Any of the residents with extraordinary abilities could be watching me, or at least sending energy my way. It was more likely that as I was getting more aware of my abilities, that I was tuning into the energy of the others like me. I couldn't decide if I liked the sensation.

Trust

I decided to listen to my intuition. The movement around me was not my imagination. I tensed, a prickling sensation on my shoulders. I turned to my left; in case it was Seamus messing around. No one was there. It didn't feel evil or threatening.

Was this how Grandma lived? The feeling of being alive, part of something bigger? She embraced the magic in her life. Did she simply acknowledge the unseen, the paranormal and get on with life? I wish I'd paid more attention to the time I spent with her. Maybe she'd given me clues on how she dealt with this?

Whenever Mum felt the residents of Spirit Town were overly active, she would protect herself from getting caught up in whatever was going on. With a simple click of her fingers, she created a bubble around herself mentally and physically.

I clicked the fingers on my right hand. Did I expect anything to change? The agitation slowly ebbed away, replaced by a sense of calm. I felt the anticipation in the air. The town collectively waiting for what was going to happen next.

As I entered the café, Mrs Moran, who was leaving, patted me on the arm. "Good talk today, dear. I taught you well. Your voice carried right over to where I was standing. Not that I was being a sticky beak. The incident this morning, was on the way to the library, where I was headed to borrow some more books. I stopped because I wondered what the commotion was all about." I smiled at my old English teacher. I'd been in her public speaking and debating team. *Creating strong minds and voices*. I saw Lara waving from the table the furthest from the door.

"Six of the eight residents are coming at two this afternoon. Mr Elder is in hospital after a funny turn where he fell off his tractor. He's okay, according to his wife, just a little forgetful these days. Miss Haese is teaching in the city. She moved there a few months ago. The others are all keen, and excited to be on video." Lara reported.

Evie called from the counter, "I made a fresh batch of pumpkin soup. Mum baked some bread if you're interested, not gluten free, though."

"Can we have four serves of both please. And water for the table?" I glanced at Lara, who nodded. "The others should be here in a few minutes." I lined up at the counter to pay for all our meals. Evie handed me a tray with a jug of water and glasses.

All the people in the queue behind me nodded and smiled as I passed by. I returned their smiles. Familiar faces, although their names escaped me at that moment.

"Is it my imagination or is everyone extra friendly today?" I asked Lara, joining her at the table. "I mean, I know it's a friendly town, but this seems unusual."

"I don't think you're imagining it. Maybe they were at the park this morning and heard you speak?" Lara suggested.

"Here she is, our local celebrity," Seamus teased as he and Jon joined us at the table. He pressed his hands together, pretending to applaud. "Don't tell me you haven't seen the footage on social media."

"I'd forgotten about that." I turned to Lara. "Lexi told me someone filmed me talking this morning. She showed me on her mobile. I didn't give it a second thought."

"That'd explain the customers smiling and nodding at us," Lara responded.

"I'm hoping that whoever is causing the fuss will make a mistake now that I called them out as vandals. Maybe then I'll be able to catch a glimpse, with second sight, and we can solve this mystery," I said. "Oh, and I ordered us all pumpkin soup and crusty bread."

Jon and Seamus both nodded their agreement to my choice for lunch.

"How did you go at the Neilson place?" Lara asked.

"There's something strange about the place. I can't quite work it out. My spider senses were tingling," Seamus said. "The farm has a lot of machinery in their big shed, including an Ogre. They've renovated the old Anderson place. A couple of acres of potatoes and pumpkins growing. We didn't get to see all the paddocks. Clive and Margie have three teens. Despite all the mod cons, technology and machinery, it felt a little like stepping back in time."

"I agree. I don't have second sight or any special skill, but the family were definitely hiding something." Jon said. "I don't know if there our vandals. There's something in that shed they don't want people to see. A hunch isn't enough for a search warrant. Neither is having an Ogre, or a dirt bike."

"So, what's next? In terms of finding out what they are hiding?" Lara asked, as she twisted the napkin the lay beside her plate.

Seamus answered, "I know the farmers who live either side of them. The Murphys and the MacDonalds. Jon and I are going to pay both farms a visit. Ask them what they think of their neighbours. If there's been anything odd happening, that sort of thing."

Jon nodded. "The other officers have been kept busy by people thinking they saw something odd or suspicious. They are following up all the leads. I really appreciate having the extra eyes and ears with me. I know you've your own business to run." He pulled his mobile phone out of the pocket of his shirt, and read the message on the screen.

"All good, mate. My businesses can do without me for a few days. I trust the guys working for me," Seamus replied. Something about the way he spoke, reminded me of the elves his dad used to have helping them on the farm. It was so long ago; I had forgotten about them. Were they still there?

"I was telling Beth that six of the eight residents we contacted are willing to come along to an informal video catch up at two this afternoon." Lara gave the boys a brief update, lining her cutlery up to one side of her plate.

"The radio and television stations are willing to run the story once it's filmed. After Lexi checks it and makes any necessary edits," I added, just as Evie arrived with lunch. The table grew quiet, as everyone tucked into the soul-warming food in front of them.

Velvety and warm, the pumpkin soup was soothing, healing, soul food. The crusty bread melted in my mouth. Whatever the secret recipe was, she had the magic touch when it came to cooking.

As if reading my mind Seamus broke the silence. "Evie's food is as delicious as ever. Her parents are magic when it comes to food. They seem to know just the right ingredients to create a perfect meal every time."

"Am I right in guessing they have an unique gift for this sort of thing?" Lara scraped the last of her soup out of her bowl.

"Sure do. It's the one place anyone can eat, no matter what allergies we have, gluten dairy, nuts, eggs, and no one ever feels ill afterwards." Seamus picked up another piece of crusty bread, mopping up the remnants of his soup with it.

Chapter 6

The atmosphere in our meeting room was of a group of excited six-year-olds on a play date. Old friends pleased for an excuse to gossip over a cuppa and some cake.

Representatives from six local families; their ancestors in the town at least eighty years, maybe more. I sat quietly, sipping my coffee, and listened as they shared stories from their childhood. They laughed and cried as they remembered lost friends, made their cups of tea and munched away on the white chocolate and raspberry muffins.

Lexi was behind the video camera making sure that everything was perfect. I didn't hurry the group, but I did keep an eye on the clock on the wall. A tingling sense started at my toes. Was someone in the room hiding something? I watched and listened for clues.

The participants represented a good cross section of our little society. Mrs Oddy and old Mr Todd, both in their seventies, could count back a hundred and twenty years of family in the area. Mr Todd was retired, and still liked to visit the library and the school every chance he got. He was a much-loved figure in the community, despite his idiosyncrasies, which became more prevalent with age. His walking stick allowed him freedom. The arthritis that crippled his legs was threatening his hands. I assumed his children couldn't convince him an electric scooter was the way to go. He was small but determined. His presence used to command respect, and for me still did. Mrs Oddy, and her mother before her, had cleaned for many families. She probably knew a lot of the town's secrets. Rumoured to be a witch, a canny old dear, I'd never heard her gossip or speak ill of anyone. Her snow-white hair, always gathered high on top of her head, her glasses enhanced her smiling eyes. A surrogate grandma to the children in all the families she cleaned for.

Kath Wilson had grown up on the Anderson farm, before marrying and moving into town. The doctor's wife, she was privy to many town secrets. Unpretentious, she was highly regarded by most people. She had recently turned fifty, and had donated several trees to the school to create more shade for children playing outdoors. Tall and thin, her short dark hair was always immaculate. Her signature clothing, which I loved, the colourful shirts she always wore, she designed herself. Brad Arnott was similar in age. He worked at the local mill, as his father and grandfather had done before him. He still coached the junior football team. Bald, with a beer gut, I couldn't quite work out if he was genuine or not.

Simon Knox and Betty Smith were only a couple of years older than me. I had interviewed their mothers originally. Simon was the teacher librarian at the primary school, in the role occupied by his mother when I was a student there. He loved chess and ran a weekend tournament. He always wore a beret, and a grey vest. Average height and build, I suspected his clothes style was a way of standing out in a crowd. Betty had taken on her mother's hair salon when she left to travel around Australia with her sisters. Her hair was often short, spiky, and multi-coloured. I remembered a time when it was long, with ringlets. With various piercings and tattoos of frogs and butterflies, she was always smiling and laughing. The hair salon's services now included a nail technician, piercing and tattoo artistry. Sporting teams, school classrooms, family celebrations, the people assembled in this room were part of a combined history, an entwined history. I glanced at the clock. It was time to start.

"Okay everyone. I know we all have a lot of catching up to do. I'm happy for you to all stay here as long as you like after we shoot the video." Everyone stopped talking and turned me expectantly. "As Lara explained when she rang you this morning, we're shooting a promotional video for our Spirit Festival. It will be shown on television and the audio will play on the radio. If you would like to take a seat, Lara and I'll start the conversation." I took my seat beside Lara, as the others joined us at the table.

"I don't know all of you. I'm Lara. I own the health food store. Why don't we start with everyone introducing yourselves? It would be good to know a little bit about you, whatever you want to share. What do you love most about the festival? The memories you have of the festival over the years, that sort of thing. Anyone can jump in and add details. An informal chat." Lexi nodded that the camera was ready to go. "Okay, Mr Todd, why don't you start?" Lara smiled at the retired teacher.

Mrs Oddy's ability to cook anything and heal minor injuries; she was the only one gathered that I knew for sure was gifted. I didn't know how to turn my intuition on or off. If it was a lesson Grandma had taught me, it was long forgotten. My gift had always been there, then when I didn't pay attention to it, it faded, going into hibernation. As the residents spoke, I sat back in the chair; wriggled my toes and tried to read the room. Shoulders back, I aligned my core, trying to look beyond what my eyes could see. Trying not to overthink it.

Simon and Kath, if I had to choose. Something about their aura, a kind of static electricity. Could Simon make himself invisible? Moving about unseen and unnoticed? Not anything untoward, it was more like being able to move through time, to different places and eras. Not that I planned to ask him if that was his special talent. I prided myself on not being a nosy reporter, and anyway, it was none of my business. Kath's gift was more difficult to pin down. Ancient, hidden, scientific, the image of gold and wealth, conflicted with one of a lioness. The Wilson's were shape shifters, but Kath had married into the family.

I sat a little straighter, bringing my focus back to the conversation in the room. Betty was sharing her memories of the festivals when she was growing up. Before computers and the internet, when word of mouth, letterbox pamphlets and notices in shop windows were used to pass on information. Children dressed up as their favourite magical book characters for the main street parade. There were merry-go-rounds and other side shows in the park afterwards. Old fashioned show bags, with proper toys and gifts.

FORTY-FIVE MINUTES later, Lexi stopped the video and checked the tape. "You're all wonderful people." She beamed. "We've plenty of footage we can use."

"Thanks everyone. You're welcome to stay and chat. Have some more tea or coffee. Lexi will let you know when the final video is ready for viewing. We'll make sure you get copies to keep and that you know when it will air on television and the radio." I stood up and stretched. The buzz of the positive energy followed Lara and I as we left the room.

"Your idea worked beautifully," I told Lara. "I need to walk, to stretch my legs after those yummy muffins."

"Do you mind if I join you?" Lara asked, as Lexi joined us in the front office.

"Not at all," I replied.

"I'll stay here, play around with the video, and tidy up after they are finished." Lexi stated. "This was fun. Can we do more video interviews?"

"Not today." I smiled. "But yes, in the future. Just don't stay back too late. Maybe start moving them out around four if they haven't made a move by then."

"Do you need to check in at the shop?" I asked. We had automatically turned right as we left the office. The autumn wind blew a loose strand of hair across my face. I grabbed it to tuck it back into my hair tie. Windy days were part of life in Spirit Town. Something I hadn't considered for years, were these blustery weather conditions real or a result of magic? Was there a way to tell? If only there was a book that would provide the answers to all the questions I had. I wasn't about to believe what I read on the internet about such things. I took a deep breath, settling the crankiness that always rose in me when I got buffeted about by the breeze. An image of a group of small children, dancing and chanting, popped into my head. Was my second sight answering my question?

Lara's voice cut in on my thoughts. "I will, but I'm keen to see how George is going at the park." That sinking feeling in my stomach returned when she mentioned George. I had forgotten to talk to him about my words earlier in the day. Before I could answer Lara, a group of children ran past, laughing and giggling as gusts of wind propelled them along. Their faces recognisable from my vision a few seconds earlier.

GEORGE LOOKED UP AS Lara and I approached. Kneeling in the middle of the garden bed full of geraniums, gerberas and roses, he was planting a purple daisy bush.

"The garden is looking great George, even better than before," I told him. I meant it. The vibrancy of the yellows, purples, oranges and reds, and their sweet fragrances wafted by; there was no hint of the destruction of the previous day.

"Thanks Beth. I heard that I'm going to be creating new garden beds," George said, straightening up and stepping back onto the grass in front of the bright red geraniums.

"Yes. Sorry about that. I came to find you earlier this morning, then got distracted and forgot to ring you," I replied.

"That's okay. You're a busy lady. This is what I was thinking." He raised his arm and pointed to the area between the existing beds of flowers and the trees. "Over there, roses with marigolds underplanted. To the left, a fragrant garden. Rosemary, lavender, and pots of mint. On the opposite side we can plant some natives. What do you think?"

"I think that's an amazing plan. What do you need from me to make it happen?" I asked.

"I've already ordered all the plants from the nursery. The only thing is, Max said the council aren't paying for any additional plants. He said it was your idea, your money. Apart from that, depending on when you would like it finished, I may need another pair of hands, or two," George replied. "Sorry about Max." His voice trailed off.

I decided to let that go for now. There would be an opportunity to have words with Max. I wasn't going to make George feel worse about it than he did already. "I'll pop into the nursery and pay for the plants this afternoon. The aromatic garden is such a wonderful idea, George. Would it be possible to have the new gardens completed by the end of the week? I can organise three strong young men to help for a few hours each day." I was sure Seamus would know someone suitable who could help. "Did Max say whether he would pay you to work on the garden?"

"I'm the council gardener. I have gardening to do. I'd like to see him try to stop me working in the park," George said defiantly. "If you can give me that additional pair of hands, then by close of business Friday, the new gardens will be ready."

"Knowing our Beth, she'll want it done yesterday." Seamus and Jon arrived while we were inspecting the area George thought would make a great aromatic garden. I could see myself brushing past the herbs, releasing their healing aromas.

I ignored Seamus. "Thanks, George. I appreciate you putting in so much work and time into this. The park will look amazing." I knew I was speaking on behalf of everyone. I was determined that nothing would stop the festival going ahead.

OVER THE NEXT FEW HOURS several things happened.

As I was walking into the kitchen, the tingling that began in my fingers caused me to drop the bag of groceries I was carrying. I examined the contents for damage. There were no injuries to the milk, apples, chocolate, and strawberries. Luckily, the laptop bag slung over my shoulder hadn't been affected by the prickling sensation. Was it a warning? Did my intuition need a boost, possibly chocolate? Using all the will power I could muster, I placed the chocolate in the fridge with the other groceries.

I sat at the kitchen table with a cup of peppermint tea in front of me. Grandma always said *things made more sense with a cup of peppermint tea.* I couldn't shake the feeling that something else was about to happen.

The image that flashed in front of me was of someone lighting a fire in the gazebo at the back of the community centre. It felt like I knew the perpetrator—I just couldn't put my finger on who it was. They had their back to me. As I kept my eyes glued on the image, the scene changed. I saw the huge gates that should have been proudly heralding the entrance to our town, distinctly out of place along the wall of a huge shed. Lined up near the gates, I saw a green and yellow tractor, a red combine harvester and a green rotary cutter and hay baler. Chickens ran in and out of view. On the wall behind the gates, I made out a picture of a giant pumpkin, with a first-place ribbon.

I knew Jon had placed one of the constables on watch in the park and general main street area overnight. The added police presence might deter the culprit from causing more trouble or lighting the fire I saw with my second sight. Should I contact Jon and tell him about my vision? Could it wait until morning? As I was debating the question, my phone rang.

"Where are you?" Lara sounded odd—not panicked, but alarmed.

"At home. What's wrong?" I asked, concerned because her voice was shaking. Lara was generally quiet but didn't strike me as overly anxious or jumpy.

"Can you come down to the shop? There's a crowd in the street. They're talking about a fire somewhere in town. Jon and Seamus are on their way too."

"I'll be right there."

I parked my little hatchback behind the office. It was easier than driving through the throng of people milling around. It was a shame it wasn't a series of positive events that were bringing people out of their homes and workplaces.

Joining Jon, Seamus and Lara outside her shop, I sought confirmation of my vision. "Please tell me the fire was at the back of the community centre."

They looked at me oddly. Jon answered, "Yes, in the gazebo at the back of the centre." He looked exasperated. "I don't know why the crowd decided to gather here, in the street. At least they aren't in the way of the emergency services."

"Maybe because they decided to order dinner from the café? I know I would." Seamus rubbed his tummy, feigning hunger.

Seamus was probably right. Of the people that were standing around, I watched as a few walked slowly to the café. Others wandered back to their cars. Mayor Max was nowhere to be seen. I walked to where a group of locals were standing, their frowns and creased foreheads giving away their concern.

"The incidents of the last few days are a little scary. I'm certain the police will find and stop whoever is committing the crimes. The best thing we can do is to go home and engage in whatever activities we'd normally do. Whoever is doing this wants a reaction. If we don't react, they'll get bored and stop behaving badly." I didn't know whether I believed my own words, but I had to do something. Most of the group nodded. I got a few tiny, nervous smiles as they dispersed. A few wandered into the café, the others to the supermarket or to parked cars.

"I could use a coffee." Jon sighed. "Does anyone want to join me?"

Agreeing that coffee sounded like a good idea, we joined the line into the café. I ordered four coffees and some toasted sandwiches, while the others grabbed one of the free booths. Evie was busy with the additional customers. She served everyone with a smile. "You look like you could use this," she said, bringing our food to the table. We nodded our thanks as she hurried back serve the rest of the meals.

The events of the last few days were weighing heavily on us. Seamus was quieter than usual. He was less enthusiastic about food, which wasn't like him at all. Lara was drumming the table quietly with the fingers of her right hand. I didn't know her well, but I had a few nervous tics of my own. I concentrated on keeping my tapping foot still. My leg had a habit of moving involuntarily whenever I sat for long periods. I didn't want to add to the nervous energy that was threatening to consume our town. Jon had his notepad out, flipping through the pages. I wondered how many pages of notes he had written since Monday.

"How did you know the fire was in the gazebo?" Jon asked as I took a bite of my sandwich. I chewed the mouthful quickly. Swallowing, it caught in my throat, scratching on its way down.

"A vision. My second sight, I guess. Just before Lara rang. A figure starting the fire in the gazebo. I couldn't make out who it was." Placing my sandwich back on the plate I asked, "Did you get to see inside the Neilson's farm shed?"

"Not really," Jon admitted. "We didn't have a reason to. Why do you ask?"

"A second vision—a farm shed, with a tractor, combine harvester and other equipment. The gates were standing in the corner. There was an award for a prized pumpkin. I'm not saying it's the Neilson's place. Most farms probably have prizes, and farm equipment. As I say this out loud, it does sound lame."

"Did you see anything else?" Lara asked.

"Just the fire, and then the farm." I looked over to Seamus. "You have mates with some unusual gifts. Would any of them have an idea what is going on? I don't mean I think your friends are the vandals, but maybe they know who is."

"I know what you mean. There are a few of us who keep in touch, kick the ball around a couple of times a month. None of them would be responsible for this mess, but yeah, they might know something. We're due to catch up. I'll let you know if they mention anything," he said to Jon.

"Has anyone heard from Max, or Juliet?" Lara asked. "We were supposed to catch up for a chat, but she didn't show. She isn't answering my texts."

"Max is probably keeping her busy. To stop her talking to us," I mused. "I haven't heard from either of them. Maybe we'll be summoned to another meeting tomorrow."

"On that sobering thought, I'm heading back to the station." Jon stood up. "Someone in town knows what is going on. This mystery isn't going to solve itself."

"A great first week," Seamus commented as we watched Jon leave. Lara and I nodded.

Lara covered her mouth with her hand as a yawn escaped her lips. "Sorry about that. I'm going to check the shop and head home."

"Good idea." Seamus and I followed Lara. We turned to wave goodbye to Evie as we pushed open the door. There were still customers seated, finishing their meals. Evie was wiping down the empty booths, with no more customers waiting for food. By the time Evie was ready to leave work for the day, I'd be tucked up in bed, grateful that I hadn't chosen hospitality as a career.

Chapter 7

I held my breath and turned on the radio, exhaling a few seconds later when Thursday morning's early news failed to mention any incidents in Spirit Town. The migraine that had been lurking around the edges for the last few days decided today was the day to kick in. I couldn't remember the last time I had taken any kind of leave. It would have been in my job in the city before I was the one everyone relied on. At least that was how I felt. Responsible. To make sure my parent's businesses were successful. Lexi was quite capable but still I felt responsible for her as part of my team. In some weird way I also felt responsible for making sure our little village was a safe place for everyone and that we were all able to enjoy the festival, without the weird goings on.

A few more minutes in bed wouldn't hurt. The pounding on the spot right between my eyes confirmed I made the correct decision.

I sent a quick text to Lexi, Lara, Seamus and Jon, in case I slept through the alarm I was about to set.

Working at home today. Let me know if you need anything.

Taking my cup of coffee, I returned to my bedroom. I tried to read the latest news. My eyes ached too much. I sighed, closed my laptop, and lay flat on the bed. It wasn't cold enough to pull up the covers. I hated succumbing to illness, but to beat this migraine I had to give my eyes a chance to rest.

Opening my eyes after what felt like a few minutes, the light coming in from the window told a different story. My phone confirmed it was nearly half past ten. I'd slept through the alarm I'd set for nine. I closed my eyes. Just for a few minutes I told myself.

It was nearly two in the afternoon when I finally climbed back out of bed. The pounding in my head had all but vanished. Tipping my cold coffee into the sink, I filled the kettle and turned it on.

I checked my emails while I drank my cuppa and munched on an apple. Remembering the strawberries, I polished them off too.

I read Lexi's email first. The video was ready; the radio and television station were both going to run the story the next day. Lexi had spoken to Lara, and they had contacted the participants and sent them copies of the video. The next addition of the paper was under control.

Lexi had worked with me for long enough to know that if I was working from home, I needed peace and quiet, or I wasn't feeling well. I knew her well enough to know she was capable of running things by herself for a few days.

The next email, an ambiguous one from Max, addressed to everyone on the festival committee simply said, "I want a full report by the end of the week." It wasn't written in capitals, but still felt like he was yelling at us. I deleted the email.

There was only one text on my mobile. Lara checking in to see if I was okay. *I am now. I had a migraine earlier.*

No residue or lingering pain; my decision to sleep it away had been effective. My restless legs led me outside to where Buddy was patiently waiting.

"The thing is," I told him, feeding him half my second apple, "if I want to solve this mystery, then I have to do something differently. Step out of my comfort zone. That's what Mum and Dad would tell me." His beautiful, soft, loving eyes met mine. It was easy to trust animals. People I don't tend to trust or forgive easily. Maybe I needed to forgive myself first. "If I want my second sight to work properly, I should go straight to the people who can help me." The thought of attending the regular Thursday evening meeting was nearly enough to bring my migraine back.

The last time I attended one of the gifted community weekly meetings, I was a teenager. An unpleasant encounter with a group of other young people, the situation didn't end well. "I haven't told another living being, Buddy. We were young. Experimenting to see what our abilities could do. Someone was injured. Everyone else ran away and I was blamed for what happened." Though the accident wasn't my fault, I stopped using my abilities. Embarrassment, pride, and other emotions far too complicated to name. I left town soon afterwards.

"I'll bring you some more treats tomorrow," I promised Buddy as I left him munching on some clover. A dull ache, as if someone poked me in the middle of my shoulder blades, caused me to stop at the back door. I turned around. There was nothing odd hiding in the back garden; Buddy kept the grass at a reasonable level. I wasn't sure what I expected to find— a withered hand pointing in the direction of the culprit?

I found the tight spot and gently massaged it. The pain eased a little. Stretching my neck, arms, and legs, using the old chair on the back verandah, I loosened the tight muscle.

Trepidation at the thought of attending the meeting made my palms sweaty. Fifteen years ago, it had been intriguing, interesting and a little entertaining. Curiosity at the extent of our abilities kept me attending. I looked back on the memory as a movie, rather than something that happened to me.

There had been ten of us that night, all excited at learning how to manipulate the world around us. I refused to direct my energy to any one person or living being. Seamus was absent that day, attending his grandfather's wake, or he would have stood by me. The others laughed at me. I walked away. The next morning, I heard about the accident when the police called to question me. I refused to name anyone They had all given statements that I'd used my ability to cause a car to drive off the bridge. No one was killed, but three people spent time in hospital. There was no actual proof, and no charges were laid.

Looking back at that time, with the benefit of hindsight. I could've been more of a joiner. I was curious about my powers but had no people skills. Being Seamus's friend was easy, but otherwise I chose my own company. Mum and Dad never encouraged the power side of things. Grandma taught me what I knew. The excitement and energy of the others had been contagious that night, Not so much that I'd use my powers for maliciousness though. No wonder they made me the scapegoat. I would have too. I guess my parents had the most influence in the town, so they figured I'd be okay.

I didn't know if my old classmates were still living locally. The law of averages would indicate some must be, while others had moved on. I shivered. Not looking forward to seeing them again, but this was something I wanted to do.

YOU CAN DO IT BETH, I told myself as I got ready. What was I scared of? I was a grown woman. I wasn't letting anyone manipulate me.

The location was the old church near the cemetery at the edge of town, abandoned after floods damaged the foundations. The town built a new church on higher ground, leaving the old structure as an historical landmark. My parents' generation, those with special abilities, spent weeks restabilising the building. The council offered it to the group as a safe place to hold their meetings. The protection spell surrounding the property allowed tourists and locals to visit and view the building from the outside. They could take photos and wander around the building and not see anything other than an old run-down rustic church.

I knew they still met there most Thursday nights. The time and place never changed, so that all with extraordinary abilities knew there was a safe place if we needed one.

I disagreed with the craft nights—learning spellcraft, witchcraft, astral traveling, invisibility. The talents across the community were varied. After what happened to me, I knew what happened when people used the skills for the wrong reasons: to manipulate the elements, people and situations. I shuddered.

I remembered my first and last weather spell. How was I supposed to know that the lightning would strike the old wooden bridge at the precise moment that Peter Wells was taking his cattle to the long paddock? While Peter wasn't hurt, he wasn't able to rescue all his cattle. He packed up and left Spirit Town not long afterwards.

I wasn't the only teenager who chose to test their magic powers. I could write a book about the Spirit Town mysteries—the purple trees, the river becoming raspberry cordial, firecracker like lights appearing suddenly and randomly throughout the town, the school that disappeared for a week.

Part of me wanted to text Seamus and ask him to join me. To admit that I had no idea how to fix my second sight. That I decided to swallow my pride and attend the meeting. Something stopped me. This I had to do by myself. The rule was that we were always welcome, unless we'd been exiled and no longer lived in town. I might be scared, but I would be safe.

I drove to the church. I didn't mind long walks, but I wanted a quick escape in case it was needed. The last thing I wanted to do was offend the group, which might happen if I spoke too much. I parked on the street near the cemetery, tempted to check if the council had made the repairs. If I entered the cemetery, I might lose my nerve and not attend the gathering. Keeping my head down, to keep myself as invisible as possible, I entered the church.

A few people turned to see who had entered the building, but within seconds returned to their conversations. I tried not to view everyone with suspicion and distrust. Most of those in attendance would be able to read my thoughts.

I found a spare seat and sat down, smiling to those who acknowledged me. A few seconds later, all eyes turned to the person at the front of the room. Mrs Marigold held up her wand in one hand and a dream catcher in the other.

"How many of us remember our dreams? Are our dreams prophetic? Second sight— do we use it to its fullest capacity?" Each sentence was short and punchy, delivered in her serious teacher's voice that sent shivers along my shoulder blades. "The trick is to prepare ourselves properly for our dreams, and to engage with our visions. To practise second sight, we must believe in our abilities. Tonight, we will be working in pairs. To learn and practise some simple steps to align our confidence with our abilities. The key to seeing is believing."

Did Mrs Marigold know why I was here? Was this lesson planned all along or a direct result of my attendance? I felt nauseous. My stomach turned itself inside out. On one hand I desperately wanted to learn more—on the other hand I was too scared to give it a go. While people were choosing who they wanted to work with, I slowly and somewhat reluctantly left via the closest side door. I sensed eyes watching me. Mrs Marigold's eyes burning hotter than the others. She intimidated me, but I was more fearful of my own powers. I locked my car as soon as I jumped in the driver's seat. Trying to focus only on the road ahead I drove carefully home.

I COULDN'T SETTLE, cranky at myself for leaving the meeting early. Why didn't I just get over my fear, forgive myself and learn some stuff? I wasn't the only gifted teenager to make a mistake. No one else cared, why did I? The lesson had been exactly what I wanted to know. My shoulders tingled. Eyes burnt holes in my back. I spun around. The burn felt real, as if I'd sat too close to an open fire or scalded myself with hot water. No one was behind me. No one I could see. I moved around my kitchen, shaking away the residual energy from the gathering. Special abilities came with a price. One of mine was picking up the energy, feelings, and emotions of others. I fiddled with the clear quartz bracelet I wore on my wrist for protection. One of the lessons from Grandma that for some reason I always heeded. Not that I ever thought about protection when I wore it. The bracelet was merely a reminder of time spent with her. A few deep breaths would normally clear my energy, except that I'd just spent some time in a room full of people who could manipulate energy and the elements. My heart was still wildly thumping in my chest. At least the nausea had eased. I reached into the drawer at the bottom of my fridge, hoping for some ice cream. The freezer compartment was empty.

My mobile buzzed in my back pocket. I jumped, nearly hitting my head on the fridge. "Hello?" I hoped I didn't sound as scared as I felt. I took a couple of slow breaths to calm my jitters.

"Beth, are you okay?"

I slumped into a kitchen chair, relieved to hear Lara's voice on the end of the phone.

"Lara, hi. Yes, I'm fine. Just a little low in sugar. I don't suppose you feel like picking up a tub of peppermint chocolate ice cream and sharing it with me?" My hands stopped shaking. Hearing Lara's voice calmed me a little.

Pull yourself together, I told the woman reflected in the kitchen window, fiddling with my bun in an attempt to capture all the fly-away straggly bits. Did the grey hairs really make me seem more intelligent? I smiled at my reflection. Mum used to tell me that with grey hairs came wisdom. If only that were true.

Hearing laughter on the front steps, I opened the door to find Lara, Seamus and Jon. "Look who I ran into in the supermarket. We bought chocolate muffins, nachos and the ice cream." Lara held up two shopping bags.

"Wine and beers too." Seamus held up another bag.

"Let's sit out on the front porch. I'll bring out crockery and cutlery." I grinned, my fear and anxiety melting away at the sight of my friends. "My day was wiped out by a migraine. I slept most of it away. So please, fill me in. Did I miss anything exciting?" I briefly considered telling them about my afternoon but decided against it. I wasn't ready to share my story yet.

OGRES AND FAIRIES. Swirling around in autumn leaves. Witches and raging rivers. Fires and lightning strikes. Giant gates and pumpkins, potatoes and ... I sat up in bed as if jolted by one of the lightning strikes in my dreams.

My sheets were soaked with sweat. I found my blankets in a tangle at the end of the bed. Were these nightmares or visions or was something more sinister haunting my dreams? In my dazed state I tried to find my cat, Guiness, the black stray who decided he belonged to our family for fifteen years. His passing was nearly twenty years ago. I'd told myself then and many times since, that I didn't need another pet. Too much trouble and responsibility. Buddy didn't count. He was easy. He kept the lawn nice and low, which saved me mowing it. In this moment I craved a pet to snuggle on the blanket at the end of my bed.

After we solved this mystery I would consider getting another feline companion. The clock said it was only 4 am. I wouldn't be going back to sleep anytime soon. I swung my legs out of bed, flinching a little as my feet hit the cold floorboards. Through the kitchen window trees stood sentry, a layer of protection as the moon light casting weird shadows in the garden, a coincidence—my nightmare on the night after I tried to repair my wonky second sight.

As a small child, my dreams had scared me. Mum taught me a rhyme to keep the nightmares at bay.

Bad dreams must go away, only my sweet dreams can stay.

Over the years, I inadvertently kept pushing my dreams away. I mused over Mrs Marigold's words—that second sight depended on belief in our ability. It made sense.

I recalled another conversation with my parents when I got distracted instead of concentrating on my studies. The art of focus. Making my cup of coffee. Rinsing the kettle and filling it up with cold water. Carefully unscrewing the lid of the jar that held the precious coffee grains. Choosing a clean teaspoon, gently and carefully picking up the coffee grains. Move the spoon slowly to the cup. My cup with cats on the side. Slowly pouring the hot water in. Watching it swirl around as it mixed with the grains of coffee. Next was the milk. Not too much to make it milky. Not too little or it's too hot to drink. Stirring in a clockwise direction. Setting intentions for a productive day. Solving the mystery. Getting the festival back on track. Getting back on track for a normal day. That would be nice.

I DECIDED TO PUT THE extra time before work to good use. Something about the previous evening was niggling at the back of my mind. Apart from the annoying aspect of teaching people with supernatural abilities even more powers. The words magic, wizard or witch invoked images of fantasy and make-believe. There was nothing imaginary about the extraordinary talents of some of our residents. Mrs Marigold teaching how to levitate, or make something disappear, wasn't an illusion. It wasn't a magic trick or sleight of hand.

Were any of the attendees our vandals? I typed up as much detail I could about the people who I saw in the church. The information might come in handy.

Kim Smith and Jay Wills could move objects, making them vanish. Jamie and Tanya Brown were able to make themselves invisible. Miranda Green and her family could cause and heal illnesses. Janet Gray and Rob, her son, created illusions. Maggie Rose had the local apothecary, way before health foods became a fad. Her ability to mix potions and lotions was known far and wide. The Underwoods were able to morph into foxes, horses, and other animals. The Steven's clan had a mix set of abilities; I wasn't sure what they were best known for. Mrs Agnes Marigold, a favourite teacher of mine in primary school, now taught magic skills.

Chapter 8

"The television station is running the story this morning, again at lunchtime and on the evening news. The radio station is going to run the audio a few times today and over the weekend." Lexi updated me on the previous day's activities. "The festival insert arrived from the printers. It will go out with Tuesday's edition. I took some stills of the group the other day and I wrote an article for next week's paper. Some of the stories from residents, what they love about the festival. Keeping the focus positive," Lexi said. "I have drafted an updated plan for the two weeks."

"That's great! I'm feeling optimistic that we have seen the end of the vandalism. The media campaign should generate excitement, something to look forward to." I looked around our office area. Our front window faced the street. All you could see from outside was our front counter and a random chair for clients to sit on.

"We could decorate our window area." I looked questioningly at Lexi. "Any ideas?" The witchy theme gave us a lot of scope. I wasn't the artistic one. With words I could weave a story, images were more Lexi's forte.

"I have a cast iron campfire pot that looks a like bit like a cauldron. We could add a straw broom and some autumn leaves." Lexi walked over to the area in front of the counter and looked up. "I think we could hang some black curtains. Tack black material on the ceiling and pin a moon and some stars on it. What do you think?"

"I think it's a terrific plan. Just tell me what you want me to do."

Before Lexi could answer, the front door swung open, banging against the wall. I had my back to it and spun around to see who slammed the door.

"Sorry, I forgot I was going to fix that door stop." Seamus crashed in, checking behind the door to make sure he hadn't damaged anything. "Beth, you need to come and see this. Hi Lexi, I'll bring her back soon. Unless you want to come too. Maybe come anyway, with your camera."

It was unusual to see Seamus rattled. Normally he was the calm one, but when he did get upset, his emotions reverberated through his whole body. His car was at the kerb right outside the office, with the engine running. Lexi and I hopped into the ute. A sense of foreboding quickly descended as we sat in silence. Seamus drove to a bend in the river, a location that was popular amongst the locals who liked a spot of fishing. Jon had cordoned off an area with police tape. Lexi and I gasped simultaneously when we saw the problem. The makeshift jetty, erected in preparation for the river boat competition had been demolished. Pieces of wood from the boat launch were floating in the river. As we walked closer to the area, I noticed the large tyre tracks.

"It's probably that same truck, the Ogre," Seamus said glumly. I could sense the anger building up inside my friend. He didn't attempt to hide it. "I mean, the gall of some people. This is easy to fix. That's not the point. We can't monitor everywhere, and we still have no idea who is doing this or why."

I put my hand on his right arm, a calming technique that had worked before. Seamus glanced at me and took a deep breath in. He held it for a few seconds and exhaled.

Lexi excused herself and wandered downstream a little. I knew she would be literally looking for a positive angle, to take photographs.

Jon walked over to Seamus and me. "This is getting serious. Someone could injure themselves if they jump in without paying attention. I'm not confident we'll be able to retrieve all the pieces of wood. At least not immediately. Max has already yelled at me, from the comfort of his office, that we must cancel the festival. I keep hanging up on him. It's not my job to make that decision." Jon shrugged his shoulders. "My boss wants to send more officers. I'm not sure that will help. Fred, Myra and Jack are doing the best they can. We sleep in shifts and patrol the town. We'll have to widen our patrol area now. What else can we do?"

"The question is, what else can we do to help you?" I asked. "We could cancel the festival and that might stop the incidents. That's not my preference."

"Mine either, I want to catch the culprits," Jon agreed with me.

Seamus pointed to the tyre tracks. "What are the chances of finding an Ogre with river mud on its tyres? Or one that has just been washed clean?"

Finches and magpies, calling to their mates, warbled in their singsong voice amongst the eucalypts and wattles. Wasps and butterflies wove and dove in and around us, unconcerned at our presence. If you ignored the demolished jetty, the river flat was a beautiful slice of Aussie bush.

Lexi joined us. "I have a crazy idea. Rather than report the destruction, can we post that the committee decided that the river was too nice a place to have the boats launch from? That instead of ruining the beautiful area, the boat race will go ahead on dry land. *Wave your witchy wand, add some wheels to your creation and join us as we sail around the racetrack.*"

"That's brilliant," I replied. "Embracing the witchy aspect is something we could focus on."

"Yay!" I could hear the excitement in her voice. "I think the radio and television stations would support this. A bit of fun instead of more drama."

I nodded. "I'll run it by the committee, but I am sure they'll agree."

"It sounds like you two witches are concocting a story." Seamus appeared more like his normal self. I was glad. "I'll drive you ladies back into town." He turned to Jon, "I'll be back with a couple of helpers to get the site as safe as we can."

Jon nodded. "Thanks, I'd appreciate that."

"I'll email Max and tell him everything is under control, that the festival is on track," I added as we hopped in the truck. Emailing the mayor was the least I could do. Mrs Marigold's words rang in my ears. What we needed was for me to believe in my abilities.

I EMAILED MAX. LEXI ducked home to see what she had at home to decorate the office. My next email was to Sharon and Izzie, thanking them for running our story and that we would send photographs promoting the festival in the next day or so. Lastly to the committee members with Lexi's suggestion of the change in venue for the boat race.

"Come and see what I found!" Lexi called from the front office. I helped her drag in a big box from the footpath. "Can you please grab the broom and the cauldron thingy—they're just outside the door," she asked as she started pulling items from the box.

The millet broom handle looked just like an old tree branch. "A perfect witchy broom," I marvelled as I placed it against the counter. "People will see it here, if they're looking in the window."

"Exactly." Lexi's eyes sparkled as she pulled a lump of black out of the box, with what looked like cobwebs clinging to some of it.

I dragged the heavy cauldron over to the broom. I jumped, nearly hitting my head on the benchtop, as a blast of eighties music erupted in the office. Lexi giggled, holding up her mobile. "Lightening the mood."

We unwound the big pile of black fabric. I hung the curtain on the rod above the window blinds. It was nearly a perfect fit, hovering just above the floor. The material only covered one half of the window which was perfect as we wanted people to be able to see our display.

Lexi stood on one of the stools, thumb tacks in one hand, a length of black material in the other. She pinned the material so that it flowed down from a point above her desk, into the top of the cauldron. A white cotton web of tiny spiders crawling into, or out of, the witch's pot. "That looks brilliant," I said in quiet admiration.

"You're next." She grinned. "Take off your cardigan, please." Before I could protest, Lexi had a black cloak draped over my shoulders. She took my hair out of its standard ponytail and a black pointy witch's hat was soon resting on the top of my head. "Are you sure you don't want to wear the rest of it?" Lexi pointed to the purple and orange lacey leggings and the shiny black pointy heeled boots propped up in the box.

"Thanks, but I'm fine like this." I pulled a face, making my eyes pop, sticking out my tongue.

"Do that again so I can take a photo!" Lexi exclaimed.

I pulled my mouth into a funny grimace. Poking my tongue out, I picked up the broom, brandishing it like a weapon.

"Your turn." I pointed to the other pile of clothes on the floor. Lexi pulled the black lace tutu on, adding the colourful leggings over her thick black tights. The devil horn headband fitted perfectly between her pig tails. Whipping out a black sparkly wand from the bottom of the box, she waved it around while I took some photos.

"Selfie time!" Lexi motioned for me to join her. The black spider-filled curtain behind us, she clicked away on her mobile as we stuck some more witchy poses. "Can you send me the photos you took? I'll post on social media. I'll send them to Izzie and Sharon too."

"Positive promotion, a good news story, and a little bit of fun," I agreed. "Just what we need."

"I didn't realise that you took a video too." I scrolled through the images half an hour later. The photos and video of me, dressed all in black, cackling and waving the broom, had received fifty-three likes within fifteen minutes of being posted.

"We can add the photos to the feature in Tuesday's edition of the paper. I hope you don't mind, I printed off some photos. We could ask Lara and Seamus if they would stick them up in their shop windows."

"Let's make it a challenge, to dress up and post photos. What about a prize as an added incentive? Dress up as our town's fictional *Spirit Witch* for a chance to win a voucher to spend locally. The newspaper will donate vouchers for first, second and third prize?" Lexi's spirit of fun was contagious. "Why don't we close early? We can put a sign in the window directing people to our webpage or email."

"Sounds good to me. Can you remind me again, what's the story behind the *Spirit Witch?*"

I tried to remember the story my grandma used to tell me. "The spirited in our community have never tried to hide their presence, but they don't advertise it either. Spirit Town was always a haven for those with unique gifts. There's a hidden veil that protects those with powers; but people can come and go and find our town. Somehow, for those who live here, gifted or not, we all tend to accept that odd or strange things happen from time to time. One of the bedtime stories we learnt as children was about the *Spirit Town Witch*. She sat in her mysterious cottage at the edge of our village, weaving the spell that keeps us all safe, hidden in plain sight." I hadn't thought about that story for years, yet it was like grandma was sitting beside me, weaving the image of the witch for me as I spoke. "As kids, we all thought we knew who the Spirit Town Witch was. Every generation suspects some old lady around here. Truth is, if we do have a real Spirit Town Witch, it's probably the last person we'd think it was."

"I love it." Lexi clapped her hands. "Can I write about her when I pose the challenge to dress up?"

"Of course. Part of our campaign of positivity."

As I stuck our sign to the glass door, Lexi shrieked, "We have over a hundred views and likes already!" I'm at least ten years older than Lexi, but even I knew that was a big deal. Our plan was working. People were focusing on the imaginary, make believe and fun aspect of our festival. "I'll monitor the comments and posts over the weekend. I might even find some more magical items to photograph." Lexi wasn't gifted as such, but her creativity was phenomenal.

"How about coffee and cake, my treat, before you head home?" I suggested.

"Sure, why not," Lexi agreed.

"What mischief are you two ladies up to?" Seamus met us at the café door.

"A well-deserved treat," I responded.

"According to social media, all you two have done all day is dress up and take photos. Seeing as you suggested food, I'll join you. I'll just go and see if Lara and Jon can join us." Before Lexi or I had a chance to reply, he bounced away down the path towards Lara's store.

"I hope you don't mind," I said as I opened the door.

"The more the merrier." Lexi shrugged with a smile.

According to my count there were seven tables with families enjoying Evie's Friday special of pancakes, scones, jam and cream. "That looks too yummy not to order. Are you happy with pancakes and scones?"

"Definitely!" Lexi clapped her hands, her eyes sparkling with excitement.

"You like caramel thick shakes too, don't you?" Remembering the last time we shared lunch, celebrating Lexi's birthday.

"I'd better order enough of your specials for five of us please Evie. Two caramel thick shakes as well please."

Evie nodded, making a note on the paper in front of her.

"You're turning into a local celebrity." Evie grinned. "That video of you the other day, and now in fancy dress. A lot of customers have been suggesting you should be our mayor. Our town spokesperson. Max has been noticeably absent."

"She's right," Seamus said from behind me. "Three chocolate milkshakes please, Evie." He walked back to the table with me. "Seriously though, you and Lexi need to be careful in case they target you next," he cautioned me. "Whoever's causing the trouble doesn't want the festival to go ahead. If you two continue to actively promote the event, well, I just want you to be careful."

'Thanks, we won't be walking down any dark alleys or anything." I could see by his frown that Seamus wasn't impressed at my jovial attitude. "Lexi is away with her parents this weekend. I'll be fine. Mum and Dad put in a decent security system. You know that," I reassured him. We both knew that system was over fifteen years old. What I hoped he didn't know it that it stopped working years ago and I hadn't yet gotten around to fixing it.

"I love the photos." Lara smiled as I sat down in the booth opposite her.

"What photos? What have I missed?" Jon asked. Lexi showed him the photos she had taken earlier.

I WOKE UP WITH A JOLT. My dreams were woven with an eerie enchantress, goblins and other mischievous creatures. Crashing through the bush near the river where the boat ramp had been demolished. Chasing me. My feet ached, throbbing as if they had run and tumbled through the thick undergrowth. I ran a shower, planning on the water washing over me, rinsing away the residue of the dream. The palms of my hands stung as I stood in the shower. I surprised to see faint scratches on them, and the back of my hands. I remembered pushing through the tea tree shrubs, to locate a safe spot to hide from my attackers. In the dream.

I shook my body, loosening the negative energy that was catching on my skin. I braced myself as I turned off the hot tap. A full burst of cold water; I forced each of my arms, my legs, and my whole body under the water. A trick mum had taught me, dissolving the remnants of the psychic attack.

My tummy grumbled, reminding me that I hadn't eaten much the previous evening. *Time for a cuppa before I feed Buddy*, I thought, turning on the kettle and the radio.

The mystery of the missing gates deepens. Stay tuned as we continue to update you, live from Spirit Town.

I only caught the end of the radio announcer's sentence. Before I could figure out what he was referring to, my phone rang.

"Morning." I recognised Jon voice instantly. "I'm out the front of your place. With coffee. Are you decent?"

"I've been awake for hours," I retorted.

"Can you come for a drive? I need to show you something." I arrived at his car and had the door open before Jon finished his last sentence.

"Morning to you too. I just caught the end of the radio news. Something about our gates?"

"Yes," Jon responded. "They came back."

I watched Jon as he drove away from the curb. The concentration, eyes straight ahead, the slight furrow of his brow, hands firm on the wheel. I sensed there was more. He wasn't in a mood to talk, that was obvious, so I sipped my coffee as he drove the two kilometres to the outskirts of the town.

"Thanks for the coffee," I prompted. Jon just nodded.

Our town gates, standing just over seven feet tall, had been returned. A crowd was gathering around the gates. "The gates are back!" I repeated what Jon had told me a few minutes before. It was worth noting for myself.

"Yeah, overnight sometime. We were patrolling as best we could, but we missed the whole thing. There is one problem," Jon finally spoke as he parked a few metres from the crowd.

As I hopped out of the car, I noticed that the gates, while they were back at the position where they normally stood, were closed. There was no way a car could drive into town on this road.

"How do we move the gates? They're really heavy. This isn't the only way into town, although it's the most used route. Whoever did this isn't stopping everyone entering or leaving town, just making it inconvenient. I guess many people would just turn back. Not everyone would persist and go around the other side of the river." My mind was spinning.

"That's the thing," Jon answered. "It looks like the gates are standing up, on their own. They don't appear to be tied to anything or jammed into the ground. They should technically just fall over. We haven't been able to move them."

"So magic is the cause for the unnatural position of the gates?" I pondered. "I don't believe I'm going to suggest this, have you considered asking someone with special abilities to help move the gates?"

Seamus walked up to join us. "I had the same thought. Do you remember Mark Stevens from school? We keep in contact. He's made a living moving heavy objects. When people need things like fallen trees or broken cars taken away, they call him."

"I don't know much about the Stevens family, but if you trust him, then go ahead."

Jon nodded. Seamus took out his mobile from the pocket of his jacket, and quickly typed a message. Within seconds his phone beeped. He checked the response. "Mark will be here in ten minutes."

More cars pulled up. "Where's Max?" I asked. The mayor was absent again.

"He decided he had a very important meeting to attend and left the crowd control to Fred and me," Jon answered. "Jack stayed at the station. Myra is patrolling the town. We really are doing the best we can. Do I say yes to an offer of more resources? Is there any point, if someone is using magic? I can't believe I'm saying that magic is the cause of the incidents." He shook his head in disbelief.

"I don't like the term either," I said. "It makes it sound unbelievable. In this instance there isn't any other explanation." I watched as more cars pulled up. People were walking around the gates, their phones held up clicking photos and taking videos. I heard them talking about posting the videos to their social media. This was not the sort of attention we needed. Unless …

"I've an idea. We're going to get media attention on this one. Seeing as Max is absent, and the festival is just around the corner, would you mind if I said a few words?" My energy buzzed through my body as if I had consumed a triple shot of coffee.

"I don't see why not." Jon shrugged.

I handed Jon my mobile. "Would you mind taking a video of what I say? I know others will, but this time I'd like a copy for Lexi to use for the festival promotion."

"Yep, I can do that." Jon nodded.

"Thanks." I handed my coffee cup to Seamus, and walked over to where the crowd were discussing the impossibility of the gates position in the middle of the road.

"Hi everyone. As you can see, we're having a little issue with our gates. They seem to have been returned to the wrong position. Is it magic? All I can say is that this year our local festival is celebrating all things witch. Did a witch use magic to balance the gates here? Was it our local legendary *Spirit Witch*? Someone is coming to move the gates to their proper place in a few minutes. Don't be alarmed by anything you see. I promise you it's perfectly safe." I caught as many people's eyes as possible. "You're welcome to take pictures and videos. All I ask is you're positive when you post on social media. We welcome everyone to come and visit our beautiful town and our Spirit Festival. There is another road in that weaves around our beautiful river. Thank you all for your patience and have a great weekend." I walked back through the crowd to Seamus.

In the distance a movement caught my eye. A flash of light, as something or someone flew through the trees. The edge of the road was peppered with gum trees, so kookaburras and magpies were common. This was something else. Or was my imagination running wild?

Chapter 9

With a loud *crack* the tall, solid metal gates swung open. Autumn leaves swirled around the base of the structure as the gates slid into their correction position on either side of the road. I was mesmerised by the movement. I knew Mark and Seamus were orchestrating the scene in front of me, but it was incredible to watch. A murmuring of the people around me told me that they were just as amazed by what they witnessed. There was no rational explanation other than the use of supernatural abilities. People would be videoing the event and posting on social media. Before I could decide how I felt about that, Seamus joined me.

"That was fun, although I wasn't sure whether my skills were up to the task. Mark is going to hang around for a while, to make sure that the gates stay where they belong." He wiped his right hand across his forehead and sighed. "It's only eight o'clock. It feels like I have been awake for hours. Coffee at the café?" Seamus held out both his hands in a thumbs up gesture to Mark. Now that the gates were back in their normal position, crowd started to disperse.

"Definitely," I cheered.

"I'll try and make it a little later," Jon said. "I want to talk to Mark first. Then I need to debrief the others." He raised his left hand to rub the base of his neck.

"Lara says the café is already filling up, so she's going to save us a seat." Seamus looked up from texting on his mobile. "Do you want a lift back with me?"

"Sure." As Lexi and I followed my oldest friend to his ute, I wondered what the rest of the day would bring.

"ARE WE SAYING THAT whoever's behind the strange events is one of our gifted community?" Lara asked. "I haven't lived here long, but it surprises me to think that they'd be behind the incidents."

"I tend to agree with you. Seamus and I were talking about this on the way here. I don't think it's a gifted community thing. There's something more sinister, more underhanded to the series of events. It feels like the sabotage is aimed at the festival, that someone's behind it all, pulling the strings," I mused, sipping my mocha.

"There is something else." Seamus's tone was serious. "Mark reminded me the Neilsons are locals after all. We assumed they were new to town because they brought the old Anderson place."

Lara, Jon and I placed our mugs back on the table, each of us turning to face Seamus. "Clive Neilson's father was one of the mechanics in town. His mother was a teacher for a while. There was an incident over forty years ago. The Neilson's were accused of stealing farm machinery. Cattle went missing as well. There was a feud with some of the farmers, including the Andersons. No one could prove anything. Still the Neilsons left town."

"I remember that story." I nodded.

Jon's phone rang. He excused himself. He returned a few minutes later. "I had Jack running background checks on some of the local farmers, including the Neilsons. He just confirmed Mark's story." He said to Seamus, "While they were never formally charged because there was no evidence, everyone thought the Neilson's were guilty. They couldn't clear their name, so they packed up and moved away. Clive grew up in the city. He married a girl he met there, Margie, and they have three children. They moved back into town a couple of years ago, after one of their children got into trouble at school."

"Mark said Clive and Margie were home schooling their children. Margie owns one of the hair salons in town. She doesn't work there very often. Mark's words were that the Neilsons were flying under the radar," Seamus added.

I made a mental note to check the hair salon the next time I walked past. I knew where it was, there were only two hairdressers in town. If I ever wanted my hair cut I went to Betty's salon, as my mother had before me.

"What's the next step for the police?" I asked Jon.

That's the big question," Jon admitted, moving his last pancake around the plate with his fork. "With no definite proof or evidence, we can't just go and arrest the Neilsons."

"Clive and Margie seemed to be hiding something the other day, maybe they were just being protective of their children," Seamus said. "Could we ask some of our extra ordinary residents if they've any information about the incidents?"

"Wouldn't they have already come forward if they'd any idea who's behind the events?" Lara asked.

I glanced at Seamus. He gave me a tiny smile, the corners of his mouth just tilting enough that I picked up on it. "Many of those with special abilities keep to themselves. They are cautious about appearing to stand out. Not everyone understands their gifts, and might blame them, in the same way we might blame young people, or a bikie gang. Those who have special abilities are just like everyone else. Some do the right thing, others may not."

"Do you have any ideas how we could go about asking the community as a group? Is there a protocol, or a specific person to talk to?" Jon asked.

"There's a weekly meeting that some of the community attend." Seamus looked at me. "I hear you called into the last gathering, how was it?"

I considered how best to answer that question. "It was interesting. I counted about twenty residents. They still meet every Thursday evening. They share stories and their crafts. If we're looking at attending the next one, that's nearly a week away."

"Could we contact the convenors and request an extraordinary meeting, for this evening or tomorrow? They may appreciate being asked and be willing to discuss or share any thoughts they have on who's responsible. We could make it clear we're not accusing anyone; we would appreciate their particular expertise to help solve the mystery," Seamus suggested.

Before anyone could answer, Jon's phone rang again. "Where? I'm on my way." Jon stood up. "You'd all better come with me."

As we opened the door to the café, we saw the problem. I counted more than a dozen cows wandering up the middle of the main street. Defecating, as cows do, and leaving a trail of muck and mud behind them. Dogs barking in the streets nearby could probably smell and hear the cattle's low mooing as they travelled though the town. Residents in town for their Saturday morning shopping were displaying a variety of reactions to this latest unusual occurrence. Mainly curiosity, or indifference. I sensed fear and even horror.

Seamus nodded at a few farmers who weren't particularly perturbed at the scene. "If we herd them to the block on the corner of Simpson and Richmond Street, we can close the gate. Then we work out who owns them."

The vacant block was only a few metres off the main street. Kev Purcell, Ken Keys and Seamus positioned themselves and gently directed the cows along the road, and in through the gate. Ken's son, Graham, drove his ute up to the fence along the west side. He hopped out with a roll of wire, checking the fence for any gaps that needed to be sealed.

"Farmers around here come prepared," Lara commented.

I nodded in agreement. "At last, a problem with a practical solution."

I wrinkled my nose; the aroma of fresh cattle dung was a little pungent. I could hear Max's voice behind me. "I don't care how much overtime costs. Get me a council street cleaner truck to Tumble Street now."

"Whoa hang on Max." Jon turned to the mayor. "Get the street cleaners to start at the corner block where the cattle are. We need to trace the trail of dung back to its point of origin so to speak. Otherwise, we won't be able to figure out where the cows came from. It might be a farmer has a broken fence and the cattle are innocent escapees."

I thought that was a great point, until Jack interrupted, "That won't work. I tried that. The mud and excrement start at the bottom of the road. As if they were dumped out the back of the truck and sent up the main street. We need to canvas the witnesses, anyone who may have seen the cattle truck."

Jon nodded gloomily. "Why isn't anything here ever straightforward? Good job, Jack. Can you and Myra get on to that please? Anyone who didn't see anything, can you gently suggest they go about their business. I'll get Fred to stay at the station and deal with any customers."

Max wandered off, muttering something under his breath about a very important meeting, and that we'd better get on top of everything soon or heads will roll. "Did he forget that apart from Jon, the rest of us are volunteers?" I said out loud to no one in particular.

Jon looked hopeful. "I take it that means you will organise that meeting with the group with the special abilities. I don't mean to use the wrong term, extraordinary, supernatural, what's the best way to refer to them?"

"I think any of those terms are fine. It's more about being inclusive and respectful," Seamus responded. "I'll look into the source of the bovine invasion."

"Thanks." Jon looked a little relieved. "I'll be busy collecting statements. Someone must have seen something."

I swallowed my trepidation and ignored that little voice reminding me I didn't want to go anywhere near that group of people. "Sure. I'll try for a meeting this afternoon, or worst case, tomorrow morning."

"Can I help in any way?" Lara asked. "I have the kids minding the store today. Pete and Ann are great with the customers, and they learn quickly." In their senior year, the twins were part of the Oddy clan. I suspected they inherited their talent for healing from their grandma.

"If Jon and Seamus don't need a hand, I'd love some moral support. Coffee and chocolate first if you're up to it," I suggested. Lara nodded. Jon waved goodbye, inundated with worried townspeople who wanted to know whose idea it was to traipse cattle through the town.

Before I could mention that I didn't have contact details for the group, I felt Lara's hand on my arm. I turned to see what the problem was. Our path ahead was blocked by three people in animated conversation. Mrs Marigold, Mrs Wiley, and Mr Moore turned to stare at us. I tried hard to ignore the sickening prickling on the back of my neck. I told myself to be sensible. I wasn't in any danger. Plus, for some reason I couldn't quite work out right now, these were the exact people we needed to talk to. I held my bag tightly to quell my trembling hands. Pushing out calm energy with every breath, I doubted that I was fooling anyone.

"Before you ask, young Miss Busybody, we didn't have anything to do with this morning's shenanigans," Mrs Wiley snarked.

"I didn't think for a minute that any of you did," I replied as politely as I could, slightly distracted by the flash of light that disappeared behind Mrs Marigold. Was she one of the families blessed with fairies? Elves and fairies had free will; some chose to help specific individuals and families. Evie's fairies kept the kitchen clean. Seamus's Dad had an elf that helped on the farm. Three sets of eyes on me. My cheeks flushed with colour. "In fact, I was just about to contact you, Mrs Marigold, to ask if we could meet with your group this afternoon. I was thinking with the variety of special talents in the group, you may be able to help us work out who's causing the trouble and why." In danger of hyperventilating, I regulated my breathing after saying my piece, as I waited for their reply. I didn't want to to attract any closer scrutiny.

"Were you now?" sneered Mrs Marigold. "I got the distinct impression you were less than impressed with the last meeting you attended. I didn't think we would see you again in a hurry."

I decided honesty to a point was my safest reply. "It's true that I was concerned to see you teaching your specific talents and skills to the others in the room. I consider each of our gifts unique to the individual. I do worry that some people mightn't know how to use their talents respectfully. Providing them with more abilities might cause trouble. Not that I've seen any evidence of that."

"The young lady makes a good point," Mr Moore said, although I didn't believe his words. "I like to think that we're all trustworthy and capable of learning and assimilating what we learn in a healthy way. After all, in regular school and university, there are topics where the knowledge could be used to make weapons of war, or poisons."

I knew I wouldn't win an argument with these three. "You make a compelling point, Mr Moore, and I think in the end you're right." I turned so I was facing all three equally. "Would you be willing to call an extra meeting this afternoon? Jon, our local police officer, Seamus, Lara, and I would like the opportunity to ask the group if anyone knows who's causing the trouble in the town."

"You have second sight, don't you?" Mrs Marigold asked. "Why haven't you been able to solve this problem yourself?"

"I don't have the training and experience with how to use my gift effectively. I'm seeing things, clues and insights in my waking hours and my dreams. The problem is I don't always understand what I'm seeing," I answered truthfully. The wellbeing of the town was a higher priority than my pride. "I came along to the meeting on Thursday to learn but my anxiety got the better of me. I guess my gift does still scare me." With no intention of ever voicing my feelings out loud to anyone, my words were just as much a surprise to me as everyone else.

Mrs Marigold looked at her friends and spoke to me directly. "I understand now. It's a painful lesson to learn—that we need community, that we can't solve our problems ourselves." Was it my imagination or did her voice soften?

Mrs Wiley's voice was stern, but it too had lost some of its edge. "We'll host the meeting at 6 o'clock this evening. Please warn whoever you bring along to be respectful. You're not to accuse anyone of anything. Some of our gathering may be a little skittish. We'll explain why you have asked to meet with us. They'll want to help." She nodded.

I knew we were dismissed. The three turned back to face each other, continuing their conversation. They didn't move to one side so we could continue along the path. I wasn't sure if that was a conscious action on their part or whether they were too focused on their discussion. I veered to my left to cross the road, rather than try to push past them. Lara followed me.

We walked the block in silence. People were gathering around the cows in the paddock. Children with their parents were pointing at the cattle, trying to get through the fence to get a closer look. Gary drove his street sweeper up the street in an attempt to clean away the remains of the mornings impromptu parade. Jon and the other police officers were chatting to people on the footpath.

With each step I took, I silently spoke two words, *thank you*. It was one of the tricks I learnt over the years. A mantra to calm me down when anxiety caused the nausea. Other mantras I'd used included *I can do it, I'm enough, I'm healthy,* and *I deserve abundance.*

Chapter 10

According to the billboard outside the café, Evie's Saturday special was a sweet chilli chicken burger with a side of sweet potato fries. The billboard advertised chocolate mud cake and cream for dessert.

"It's only 11 o'clock!" Lara broke the silence. "It feels like we've been awake for hours."

I couldn't help smiling. "That's because we've been up since before the sun came up. I'm starving. Do you want the burger and fries?"

"Definitely. The mud cake and a coffee as well. And some water," Lara added. "I mean, I own a health food shop, I wouldn't normally be eating so much café food, but it's been an unusual week." She held the door open for me.

"Two specials, two special desserts, two large coffees and some water as well, please." Evie rang up the till as I placed our order.

"It's on the house," Evie said, refusing to accept any money from me.

"Why?" I asked, trying to put the cash down next to the register.

"I know how much time and effort you've been putting into trying to solve the mystery of the cattle, the gates ... everything that's been going on in town. I'm not accepting any money from Seamus or Jon today, either. Now, go and chill, I'll bring your food and drinks over as soon as I can." I realised by the look on her face and her tone her mind was made up.

"Thank you. There's no hurry for our meals. We're happy to sit and chat," I told her. The café was busy—Saturday was the day people supported local sporting teams, caught up with families or ran errands in town.

"Evie wouldn't let me pay for our lunch," I sat in the booth opposite Lara. "She said we'd been helping with everything that has been going on and refused to accept my money. Our town benefits from her generosity in so many ways.

Did you know she donates a percentage of her takings back into the community via children's sports and supports our local ambulance station?"

"Spirit Town people are friendly and helpful. It's one of the reasons why I love it here," Lara agreed. "In larger towns people are generally less willing to put themselves out for others. They'd be worried they'd be blamed if things went wrong."

The left side of my neck twinged. Like someone had snapped a rubber band on it. I rubbed the spot with my left hand, stretching my neck over to the other side. "I never thought about it that way. I've been blaming the gifted community for things that happened a long time ago. It wasn't even really their fault. I guess I feared my own abilities, and it was easier to blame them." The other side of my neck twinged. I turned my head to the left, massaging the right side of my neck. "I made them out to be the baddies. The last thing I thought I'd do was blurt all that out to Mrs Marigold and the others." I suppressed a sigh. The throbbing in my neck was a clear indication that this week was wearing on my body as well as my emotions.

"Do you want a neck massage?" Lara asked, as I rubbed my neck, trying to release the tight knot that was rapidly forming.

"Thanks, but no. I have touch issues. I mean my body reacts badly to touch, there is an over sensitivity there that I haven't resolved yet. After the festival is over, I'll come in and grab some massage oils from your shop. I'm almost out of my supplements too." What was wrong with me today? Normally a very private person, it was as if someone had pressed a button, and I couldn't stop over sharing.

Fortunately, Evie arrived with our burgers and fries before any more words could be shared. Disregarding the option of a knife and fork, we picked up the burgers with our hands. We ate in silence. I watched the steady stream of customers—filling the tables, ordering takeaways, animatedly chatting to each other. I imagined, by the way some were waving their arms around and screwing up their noses, that they were discussing this morning's events.

If I wasn't so freaked out about the meeting this afternoon, I'd be discussing who could be trying to ruin our festival. Not many people were convinced it was all a promotional gag led by my wicked witch character. Did anyone in the café know who the perpetrators were? Was anyone in the café guilty of the acts themselves?

Scraping the last of the mud cake onto my fork, I savoured the very last bite. Draining the remaining drops of my coffee, I glanced at Lara. "I need to tell you something."

"Okay." Lara leaned forward, looking me in the eyes. After a couple of seconds, she glanced away. A technique I had used myself when interviewing people.

With the lump in my throat, it was difficult to swallow. I took a deep breath, deciding the best way to do this was to just talk. I didn't know Lara very well, but I did trust her.

"You know about my gift. Sometimes I see things before they happen, or just afterwards. The gift passed down on my mother's side. I've known I was one of those with special abilities since I was a child. My parents never made a fuss about our skills. My father taught woodwork at high school. My mother was a seamstress." I gulped down some water, hoping to dissolve the obstruction in my throat.

"I was in high school when there was a disagreement that split the town in half. Extraordinary people were being labelled magic, evil and possessed. A group of newcomers started the rumours, made up the stories, wrote to the paper, spoke on the radio. It caused a lot of trouble. It turns out the newbies were part of a corporation who wanted to create controversy and mystery to entice people to the town. They had plans to build a series of cottages on a vacant parcel of land and run haunted house mystery tours around the town. Thankfully in the end our community worked together and threw them out of town. I'm not sure if residents believe that we have wizards and witches in our town."

I paused, noting that the pain in my neck had eased. "The gifted community started up the weekly meetings as an opportunity to practise their skills and talk about the challenges of having supernatural abilities. Mum and Dad never attended. I rebelled as a teenager, and I used to go just to annoy them. A few things happened that scared me, I went away to university, graduated, and started work in the city. I returned a couple of years ago when Mum and Dad passed away. Last Thursday was the first time I attended one of their groups since I left town. I was curious to see if maybe they could help with my second sight. I didn't feel comfortable there, so I left." Lara was easy to talk to. She had let me tell my story without interruptions or questions. As I sipped my water, I tried to gauge her reaction to my story.

"Thank you for sharing your story with me. I can see how difficult that was for you." Lara's fingers twisted her paper serviette, tearing it into long thin strips. "I grew up in the city. My parents were professionals—a doctor and a lawyer. I was a latchkey child. I cooked dinner, did all the cleaning, and helped my brother with his homework. It was only when Bob's birth family came looking for him that our parents revealed that we were both adopted. Bob's family lived up north. He moved up there to get to know them. I went looking for my birth family. The clues I followed led me here, to Spirit Town. I sold my business in the city and started it up again here." Lara spoke quietly, though there weren't many customers left in the café.

"Have you found your family?" I asked. I found her story so intriguing that I momentarily forgot everything else.

"How did you go?" Jon asked as he and Seamus joined the table. They both had what looked like mud on their trousers. Seamus's boots were caked in it. The right side of Jon's shirt was creased. They looked exhausted.

The rest of Lara's story would have to wait. "Have you eaten?" I asked them.

"That's why we are here," Seamus said, heading to the counter to place their order. "Evie won't take our money," he told Jon on his return. "Something about the good work we're doing. So, I ordered us one of everything," he chuckled. No matter how tired he was, we could always count on Seamus for the comic relief.

"We met Mrs Marigold and a couple of the others in the street. They're organising the meeting in the old church at 6 o'clock tonight," Lara told them. "Did you find an owner for the cattle?"

"They didn't escape. A truck was seen, by more than one bystander, unloading the cattle at the bottom of the street. Our witnesses didn't recognise the man in the truck. None of the cows have tags in their ears, or any form of identification. I checked out the Neilson's farm. I don't know what I expected to find. It's impossible to tell if the cattle came from there." Jon wearily rubbed his forehead. "The cattle are safe for now. A couple of local farmers have donated feed for them. Another one brought in a water trough." Jon rubbed his forehead, the way I did at the start of a migraine, as Evie brought over more coffee for everyone.

Seamus took up the story. "At least the gates are back where they belong. They don't look damaged in any way. The park looks fabulous. George and the others did a stellar job. The graffiti has been removed from the footpath, and the cow dung has been washed all around the street. I'm getting used to the smell now."

Jon nodded. "Me too. Jack, Fred and Myra will take shifts monitoring the town and being at the station to field calls. We've asked for two more bodies to assist in the two weeks leading up to and including the festival. They'll arrive on Monday. Repairs of the damage to the cemetery should be completed by the middle of next week. Council is waiting for replacement head stones from the stone mason." As he drank from the mug of coffee, his features visibly relaxed. "Do you have any idea how best to run the meeting this evening?"

I responded with, "We don't. I mean, we don't run the meeting. Mrs Marigold, Mr Moore, and Mrs Wiley will. We told them what we hoped to achieve. That someone in their group may know or have seen something with regards to what has been happening in our town."

Lara agreed, "Beth made it very clear to them that we aren't accusing anyone. That we honestly don't know who's causing the trouble. We're hoping someone there has information that'll help us."

I stood up. The mud cake and coffee energy was kicking in. "I'm going for a walk to check out the new gardens in the park. Then I'm going to head home for a while. Do we want to regroup at my place at five thirty and head to the church together?"

"Sounds good to me. I'm going to check on the shop. The kids need a break. I might take them something to eat from here." Lara stood up too.

"Food's up," Seamus said as Evie served their lunch. "We'll see you later."

Jon nodded, surveying the huge plate of food in front of him.

IT WAS EARLY AFTERNOON, and there was a definite chill in the autumn air. I pulled the front of my cardigan around to keep out the cold air. Occasionally I toyed with the idea of moving somewhere warmer. I did enjoy snuggling up in a blanket in front of the fire though. As my mum used to say, *You can always warm up; it's harder to cool down.*

Seamus was right. George had created some fabulous new garden spaces. The native area was full of grevilleas, banksia, callistemons, with a wattle and a eucalypt as well. Once the trees grew a little taller, they would provide a shady area for picnics as well as homes for local birds, insects, lizards and probably bandicoots as well. The fragrant garden was amazing, the smell of peppermint, lavender, and rosemary mingling together as I brushed past the shrubs. When I was small, maybe four years old, Grandma taught me how to brush past her bushes of lavender and rosemary, releasing some of the essential oils. She explained how doing this could change our moods, cheering us up if we were sad. She showed me how to pick a peppermint leaf, crush it and inhale its aroma. We used to sit on the bench near her herb garden, just smelling the plants. We picked some of the leaves for cooking or making teas.

I made a mental note to remember to organise a few park benches for these new areas. I knew a few local businesses who would be more than happy to sponsor the project. With a critical eye, I honestly couldn't tell the garden had been vandalised only a few days ago. George had added more plants, which covered the area where the grass had been dug up.

Quickening my pace, I headed back up the main street. Jon was right, the smell of cow poo was wafting around subtly, as would freshly cut hay, or insect spray. The sort of smell that tickled your nose until you didn't really notice it anymore. As I drew closer to the cows it was a different story. Most of them were content with their temporary accommodation, munching on the grass and the hay. They didn't care where they defecated. A handful of people were hanging around, talking to the cows. I smiled. It was the kind of novelty that got people out and about. I wondered if that was the intent when they were deposited at the bottom of the street? I suspected that if the result had been to cause damage and alarm, they had missed their mark.

The last few hundred metres was always difficult. My feet appreciated arriving at my front door. I resisted the urge to sit down and chill. Instead, I headed out the back.. Buddy was pleased to see me, nudging my hand as I fed him pieces of apple and carrot. I felt my heart rate lessen. Spending time with animals and outside in the garden always calmed me—mind, body, and spirit.

Sitting on the garden bench, I rubbed the dirt off my parents' plaque. Memories of them assaulted my senses. The aroma of rose perfume, mum's favourite, mingled with the burnt sausage smell of every single barbeque.

Whispering in the trees, sharing secrets, as we used to do, snuggled on the picnic blanket. Kicking off my shoes, the grass tickled and prickled my feet. I sensed their presence in every part of the garden. The roses Dad was so proud of. Mum's native hedges around the border, creating a haven for the myriad of birds who visited our garden.

Wriggling my feet in the soil beneath the grass. *Grounding and balance, always grounding and balance if you're feeling stressed,* my mother used to say. I gasped as a sharp pain, like a literal stab, shot up my right side. Stretching up as far as I could, my hands straight above my head, loosening the muscles that were so tight. A deep breath in, sucking in as much of the air as I could, holding it until I almost choked for air. Flopping my body down, touching my toes with the tips of my fingers as I exhaled.

Over twenty years ago, when our generation discovered our powers, we all went a little crazy experimenting, pushing our strengths and powers to see the extent of our gifts. After spending time mucking around with our extraordinary abilities, most of us became adults and got on with the work life balance. The circle of life.

My parents instilled that work ethic in me. I used study and work as an excuse to focus only on the ordinary, practical side of myself. That worked ninety per cent of the time. I simply forgot I had any ability. I settled into the routine of managing my main job, and continued oversight of a couple of other local businesses I inherited from my parents. When not working, I read books, walked a lot and spent time out here with Buddy, where I felt close to my parents.

The stab in my side was a reminder that if I chose to ignore part of who I was, I wasn't balanced. Dad would poke me gently in the side and remind me that in order to find our mojo, we should stretch and challenge ourselves. Mum cautioned me against turning away from who I was. *You need to honour and respect your gifts. Use them wisely but use them.*

Nudging my hand, Buddy distracted me. Lifting me out of the rabbit warren I was going down. Reliving what happened all those years ago wasn't helpful. Especially as I was going to be back at that church in a couple of hours. I led Buddy through the first of the garden gates. Leaving him to munch on the longer patch of grass, I continued through the second gate into the vegetable garden. This gate was reinforced.

Gently laying my fingers on the rosemary plant, I asked *may I pick a few leaves from you and your friends? For a healthy, refreshing snack before a meeting.* These were living, not sentient, but that respect of and love of plants was intrinsic. I had forgotten my garden cutters, but careful not to yank the stems, I twisted a few rosemary leaves off the plant, collecting them in my free hand. With my fingernail as a sharp edge, I cut a couple of leaves from the curly parsley and a sprig of thyme.

An image of jars on the windowsill, each with a herb growing in water, flashed in my mind. Ever so carefully I pulled a piece of oregano out of the soil, shaking off the earth. I repeated the action with a piece of peppermint, with a silent *thank you* to both plants as I did so. I let the aromas of the herbs that I had grown with Grandma, waft around me, lifting my mood. I inhaled deeply.

A few steps to the left, I spied a small metal bucket. It sat next to the vegetable garden where some tiny tomatoes, rocket, lettuce, and kale had self seeded. It couldn't be the same bucket I used to collect herbs and veggies with, could it? It wasn't the strangest thing to occur recently. A quick glance inside – there wasn't much dirt and no nasties hiding in the bottom. I dropped my collection of herbs in. I was going to wash them in the kitchen sink anyway. I added two tomatoes and a couple of leaves of the wild greens. Just what I needed. Sometimes even I got sick of chocolate as a late afternoon snack.

"You stay here and enjoy the grass," I told Buddy, patting his back. I considered sharing my spoils with him, but I didn't want him thinking he could push through the fence and eat from that side of the garden.

Nourished by my home-grown salad and a big glass of water, I decided to prepare for the meeting ahead. I needed to get into the right headspace. I wandered into Grandma's room and stood in front of the mirror, forcing myself to look at the person staring back at me. Was I being too hard on the community? I knew my mistrust and suspicion were misplaced. I didn't really think we were in any danger. It was time to let go of the pain of the past. I listened for wisdom and advice. Like whispers on the wind her presence enveloped me, filling me with love. While I couldn't make out the words, it was comforting to know she was still around.

I walked into the room to the left of the kitchen. We called this space the library because it contained Mum and Dad's book collection. They read a lot. The room was full of paperbacks and hardcovers. Last year I donated over two hundred tomes to the local op shop for their charity drive. Mum and Dad would've approved. Having inherited their love of reading, the library now contained my favourite books. It was a tiny room, with a little window. I only had a vague, hazy memory of this room when it was originally used as the pantry. Sitting on my grandma's knee as a very small child. She'd sit here, amongst the bags of flour and sugar, and read. The shelves which lined most of the walls, once storing jars of picked fruits and canned vegetables, now contained books. A small mirror, no bigger than the size of a book itself, hung on the wall behind my reading chair. Catching the light it created the illusion of space, making the room appear bigger than it was.

I stood in front of the mirror. A totally different image stared back at me through the glass. My aura was a dark blue colour, with specs of red, green, and purple bouncing around. Grandma taught me the bright colours around a person revealed their emotions. As an empath I sensed moods and intentions. Auras might provide a clue as to who was committing the acts of vandalism.

I knew tonight's participants would be curious as to our intent. Showing fear and distrust was not a good way to start. Positive, calming energy was needed. I watched as my aura changed to a lighter hue, muted green and lilac. Not perfect, but better than before.

I was thankful that we wouldn't be leading the meeting. Seamus knew a little about my history with the gathering. He hadn't ruffled any feathers that I knew of, so he and Jon could ask questions. As long as I didn't have to speak, I should be able to keep my emotions in check.

"Are you hiding in the cupboard you call a library?"

"Seamus, hello I was just thinking about you." Blushing as I realised what I had said, I added, "In terms of the meeting. I think it's better if you and Jon take the lead. I'll keep my mouth shut and watch the room."

"Hmm, I'll believe that when I see it. Can I quote you on that? Keep your mouth shut indeed." He grinned. "Seriously though, yes of course. I called in to check that you were okay. It can't be easy, preparing to walk back in there. Coffee?" Seamus was boiling the water and scooping a generous teaspoon of caffeine into two cups as he asked the question.

"Thanks. I called in there the other night hoping that somehow it would fix my wonky intuition. I freaked out. They're still teaching skills like second sight, astral travel *et cetera* to the wider gifted community." I paused. "Have I been looking at this the wrong way around? I was angry for so long. They only teach those of us with abilities anyway, so we're just learning new skills, like we do at school. Maybe it isn't as bad as I think it is. What do you think, honestly?" Handing him the milk, I grabbed a packet of chocolate biscuits from the fridge.

"You know I've kept in contact with my mates from school. I don't attend the meetings often, but only because I'm not interested in learning the skills. I don't think we need to worry about their cross training, as you call it. After what happened, Mrs Marigold and the other elders developed a proper plan. Participants promise to follow a code of conduct. Anyone who behaves contrary to that code is made to leave the gathering. It's worked well for the last fifteen years. I think it's good we have the opportunity to learn about our gifts if we choose to."

I considered Seamus's words as we munched on biscuits. Chocolate biscuit and foraged greens – a balanced diet, as far as I was concerned. "That does change things," I admitted. "I probably owe them an apology. Thanks, Seamus, for the coffee and for being level-headed and sensible."

"Oh, I wouldn't go that far. It's more about being open and trusting people, until given a reason not to. I learnt that from your parents."

He was right. My parents had always given people the benefit of the doubt. Where did I get my propensity to act first and think afterwards? I wasn't as even-tempered as my parents.

Reading my mind, Seamus answered, "You're impetuous and stubborn. Your parents were too, but they managed their emotions. You can learn how to do that." It was rare for Seamus to raise a semi-serious subject. I knew he regarded my parents as family, and they thought the same of him. "You attended that meeting because you're looking for answers. There's nothing wrong asking for help," he said kindly.

"Do you think I should go in and apologise for leaving the meeting early Thursday night? Wouldn't they think that was suspicious?" I pondered the problem.

"You overthink things. Listen to your intuition. Focus on calming your energy. Work on being open to learning and listening. They will feel your energy, they'll know you're trying to do the best for the town."

I nodded. I knew he was right. "I can do that. I think I can. I'll try."

Chapter 11

Lara and I arrived at the old church at the same time as Jon and Seamus. After meeting at my place, we took two cars in case Jon was called away on police business.

I pointed out some of the features of the old building, to distract myself and calm my nerves. "See the peeling paint on the external brickwork, and where the wooden railings and floorboards on the verandah have been repaired? It looks old and unused, people passing by wouldn't give it a second thought. It doesn't look safe to enter, but it's been repaired and made safe years ago. The building is close enough for residents to walk to, yet out of the way enough not to attract any attention." I led Lara around the side of the building. Shade cloth and copper logs created a welcoming spot to sit. "That's the medicinal garden. My grandmother helped to establish the garden, donating many of the herbs that were more difficult to source." I recognised some of the plants from my grandmother's garden when I used to help her collect herbs and flowers.

The four of us walked into the church. The building felt different. Was it because I was optimistic, and open to whatever was going to occur? Now that I wasn't judging or cranky the space felt welcoming, safe. I sensed an energy of insight and wisdom I hadn't picked up on before.

"See, it's working already," whispered Seamus with a wink. Since that first day at preschool, Seamus had been able to tell what I was thinking, so it shouldn't have been a surprise now. Because I didn't value my gifts, I rarely paid attention to Seamus's. I made a note to acknowledge the extraordinary in life more often.

Gazing around the room, my eyes met Mrs Marigold's. I could have sworn she was looking at me differently—kindlier—or at least with less animosity. She was standing talking in a low voice with Mr Moore and Mrs Wiley. Seamus took Jon over and introduced him. Lara stayed in the back of the room with me. For a brief moment I considered that I was the one who'd treated the others with distrust and distain, and that they didn't feel that way at all.

The fifteen chairs were arranged in a circle. Less chairs than Thursday evening, when the chairs had been in three rows of ten. "How many people in Spirit Town are gifted?" Lara asked.

"It's difficult to say, some people stay when they reach adulthood, others leave. When I was growing up there were eight out of thirty in our class. I seem to recall that was about the average. One of the items on my list of things to research is how many people with supernatural abilities live in our town now." Just then, Mrs Marigold motioned for everyone to take their seats. Lara and I joined Jon and Seamus. Once we were seated, only two chairs remained vacant.

"Thank you everyone for attending tonight," Mrs Marigold said, waiting until everyone was still. I felt like she was talking to me directly as she continued, "For those who don't know me, I'm Agnes. Around the circle we are Mike-Mr Moore, Jackie-Mrs Wiley, Glenda. Glen, Greg, Juliet, Robyn, and Kim."

I watched two little elves as they darted out from under the stage and whisked the empty chairs out of the way. Another elf was at the tea station, pouring water into the urn, topping up the milk jug and replacing the used cups. All three were dressed in a mix of brown and green. Little jeans, high visibility shirts and cute little boots. *Don't call me cute.* The biggest of the three elves told me telepathically. A little bigger than fairies, elves in Spirit Town could be grumpy, but underneath they had a heart of gold.

"I think you all know me, I'm Seamus. This is Jon, Lara and Beth. We appreciate you meeting with us at such short notice."

Agnes nodded. "We're just as concerned about what's going on in our town as you are. Contrary to what you might think, we don't have some kind of magical power to solve this mystery." Turning to me she asked, "When did your second sight stop working?"

I was surprised at the question, and I took a few seconds to seriously consider my answer. "I don't really know because I don't normally try to use it. Sometimes I see things, but I generally don't pay any attention. A couple of days before the gates went missing a migraine started, which is a little unusual. It was only when the gates disappeared and the cemetery and the park was vandalised that I tried to focus, to figure out what was going on. The harder I tried, the more it was like someone was holding a curtain in front of me that blocked my view. I've managed to see a few little clues, but nothing that tells us exactly what is going on."

"Some of us with second sight also felt like our powers are being short circuited. I'm not sure that's connected to the incidents, at least not on purpose. We do have an idea of who may be causing at least part of what's going on." Mrs Marigold paused, looking over to Mr Moore to continue.

Mr Moore stood up. "We have no definite evidence that points to anyone, but we are willing to tell you a little bit about one of our families. The Neilsons came back to town to keep their children safe. Our newer generation are discovering their powers in a different way. It's a vivid and abrupt awakening. The cause is unknown, maybe the pandemic or the other world events." He glanced around at those seated. "We have developed a workshop to help our young people. We offered to help Margie and Clive with their children, but they refused. They don't trust anyone. They have something to do with the recent events, but they aren't leading it. Someone else is in charge."

"I have a theory," Robyn spoke up. "The Neilson children may be accidentally responsible for the damage. The parents are protecting their children. If it was my children in trouble, I'd do the same."

"Maybe they're being bullied," Glen suggested. "Teenagers can be cruel, mean. They sense weakness in others. The Neilson kids are fairly new to town. Easy targets."

"Is there anyone in particular that might be bullying them or forcing them to do the wrong thing?" Jon asked. No one offered any further insight. It struck me that those with special abilities don't magically have all the answers. They were just like everyone else.

Jon stood up. "I want to thank each of you, for coming along this evening and being open and honest with us. We appreciate it."

"We are pleased to be able to assist. We would like to see the festival go ahead. Hopefully we can help Clive, Margie and their kids," Agnes said.

"We all want the same thing," Jon reassured her and everyone else.

Kim looked around the room. I could see the concern and hesitation as she tried to speak but stopped herself, twice. Seamus noticed too. "Kim, did you want to say something? Anything at all? Whatever's said in here stays with us. We just want to get to the bottom of this."

Kim smiled a tiny smile of gratitude. "I think it's someone without powers who is manipulating the Neilsons. Someone who wants to cause problems for Spirit Town." As soon as she finished speaking, she put her head down, scuffing her feet back and forth. "Just a feeling I have."

"It does feel orchestrated, planned, rather than random," Lara said. "As if the plan is to stop the festival going ahead."

Jon nodded. "Has anything like this happened before?"

"Not like this," Agnes responded. "If we hear anything else, we'll come and see you," she told Jon.

"ARE YOU SURE YOU WANT to walk home by yourself?" I heard the concern in Lara's voice. By the time we'd helped Agnes pack away the chairs and tidy up it was dark outside.

"I'll be fine. It's not too cold, and there are streetlights nearly all the way," I pointed out. 'I love the feel of the autumn winds, the briskness in the air. I sit at my desk so much I don't spend nearly enough time moving my body."

"We could stop at the café for dinner?" Lara sounded hopeful.

"When Beth makes her mind up there's no changing it," Seamus answered for me. "I'm up for food though, if you're going to the café."

"I think we could all do with a quick debrief at the café," Jon said, focusing on me.

Knowing I was out voted, I feigned a sigh of resignation. "Okay, fine. Café it is." I hoped into Lara's little yellow hatchback. It was parked next to Seamus's farm ute.

"Last one to the café pays for dinner," Seamus suggested. Lara and I looked at each other. There was no way that Lara's car would beat Seamus's. His ute drove off while we were still getting our seat belts on.

THE BOYS BEAT US TO the café and were arguing with Evie when we entered. "We insist on paying this time. It feels like yesterday, it was so long ago, that we saved the town from a mob of wayward cattle." Seamus said dramatically with a smile. Evie pretended to be upset, throwing her arms up in mock horror. The big grin and wave as we drew closer gave her away.

Saturday evening was busy at the café. Family night, where kids ate for free if they were accompanied with an adult. We were late enough that everyone else appeared to be more than halfway through their meals. Jon and Seamus had ordered us all gourmet hotdogs, curly fries, and ginger beer.

We sat at the booth the furthest away from the large table of giggling children. I jumped right in. "If I don't say this now, chances are I'll never say it." The others looked at me with a mix of surprise and concern. Seamus tried hiding a smile. I suspect he knew what I was about to say. "I don't like admitting I'm wrong." I could sense Seamus's expression. I pushed past the embarrassment and kept going. "But I was wrong about people with special abilities. I let a bad experience over twenty years ago cloud my judgement. Tonight, I decided to be open minded. Or at least someone suggested I try to be." I smiled at Seamus. "I realised they have the same problems as everyone else, just trying to fit in and do their best." I paused. "I always thought that they chose to make a living out of being unusual, extraordinary, special. I tried so very hard to be normal. I chose to hide. They were being themselves, and not hiding." I stopped. I thought I'd feel drained and exhausted. Instead, getting all that off my chest was liberating.

"Perfect timing," Jon said, as Evie arrived with four tall glasses of ginger beer, and a platter of ham and cheese scrolls.

With a cheeky grin she told us, "The scrolls are on the house. Your main course will be here soon."

"You're amazing, Evie!" Lara called out after her.

"Thank you for sharing, Beth. That couldn't have been easy," Jon said quietly. "I still don't fully understand the dynamic of the town. It feels to me like some people don't even know there's a supernatural side to it. Or rather, they just choose to ignore it for their own sanity. The records at the station are odd, too. I've read back over fifty years of incidents, and some have initials and numbers but no great detail."

"That's because the team before you used to notate dates and initials of perpetrators, but not the details of the unusual occurrence. It was easier than trying to explain to their superiors what was going on in Spirit Town. Our family have kept a ledger going back two generations. It outlines some of the most unusual events and who was responsible. You can read it and cross reference with what you have if you're interested," Seamus offered.

"I'd love to take a look at your ledger thanks for the offer," Jon sipped his ginger beer. "I'm not sure how long it will take me to read through it all."

"No hurry at all. I'll drop them over tomorrow and keep them for as long as you need."

Evie arrived with the rest of our meal. A fairy followed her, flapping her wings, sprinkling tiny fairy stars around the space. Children giggled and clapped their hands. Evie's fairy didn't often make an appearance outside the kitchen, but when she did, everyone loved it. The chattering even louder than it was a few moments before.

There was silence at the table for a few minutes.

"Even though Mike almost confirmed that the Neilson's are likely involved, I don't want to accuse anyone until we're a hundred per cent certain, or as close to that as we can be. If they're being coerced or bullied, we must address that as well," Jon said.

"If what they said tonight was true, and I believed them," Lara said quietly, "then maybe we can reassure the Neilson's that if they're honest with us, everything will probably be okay."

"Bullying is scary. Not knowing where to turn or who to trust. I'm sure they don't want to ruin our festival," Seamus agreed.

I nodded. "After the festival maybe, we could organise a gathering to celebrate the supernatural community. Respectfully. With their input and ideas." I stopped, suddenly self-conscious. Seamus, Lara, and Jon were all looking at me.

Seamus made a face. "Good old Beth. She is stubborn and doesn't often change her mind, but when she does, whoo wee, she runs at it one hundred per cent. Seriously though, Beth, it's a great idea. Your parents would be proud."

I stood up, having had enough serious discussions and emotions today already. "Who wants some of Evie's famous caramel pecan cheesecake for dessert?"

A TINGLE OF DISCOMFORT startled me awake. I was in that middle space between being awake and a deep sleep. Eyes stared at me from the foot of my bed; I recognised them straight away. Mum and Dad visited since they passed to the other side, but not often. It'd been a while. Their images were hazy, transparent, and I couldn't make out Mum's dark green eyes, or Dad's deep blue ones. I didn't need to see them clearly. It was their presence in the room that counted.

I didn't speak, but held that connection between us; it was unbreakable, even with death the point of separation. I manoeuvred myself until I was sitting up. A wave of calmness swept over me. I didn't need to hear words, the wave of energy between us was more than enough. I lay still long after they left, savouring the feeling of peace and love that I always felt when they visited.

There were many questions, like: Why didn't they visit more often? Why did they rarely talk to me about the magical side of our family? Putting aside the fact that growing up I didn't want to know about any of it, most of the time. What was the purpose of their visit tonight?

A quick glance at my mobile confirmed I had only been asleep for a little while before the ghostly visit. Having coffee at midnight would have been a bad idea. Peppermint tea, I decided as I boiled the kettle. Standing in the kitchen, I sensed their presence. I felt the energy of the many crazy busy breakfast times we shared together. The more peaceful energy of preparations for the evening meal. Reading and talking and sharing ideas, feelings, and the good and bad about our day. I appreciated the life lessons; logical and practical, aiming high, being prepared, and focusing on work.

Sitting at the bench on the middle of the kitchen, the place of so many of these discussions, I sipped my tea.

I think you would be proud of me. Not because I can motivate a crowd, or help solve the latest mystery, but because I admitted I was wrong. I gave them a second chance. I feel lighter, and more focused, even though if I try to think logically about it, I'll give myself a headache. You did try to show me that logic and the supernatural aren't necessarily mutually exclusive. It's only taken over thirty years for me to work it out.

I sat there, sipping my tea, relishing the connection with my parents. I knew they could hear me.

My alarm clock read one o'clock when I decided I was tired enough to try to sleep. Tucking myself in under the covers, I floated on the sense of calm and peace.

The next time I opened my eyes, my phone told me it was five in the morning. I picked up the pen and notepad I kept beside the bed to jot down ideas when they came to me in the middle of the night. I wanted to capture the details that had been revealed in my dream before they faded away like clouds in the wind.

I knew from the photograph Jon had shown us, that the people I saw in my dream were the Neilsons—Clive and Margie. Maybe my ability was returning because I had made peace with the extraordinary? Did someone at the gathering unlock the blockage to my second sight? Had I unlocked it somehow?

In my vision I saw the removal and return of the gates, the graffiti, the destruction of the cemetery and the park, the release of the cows, and the fire. All the Neilson children, with Margie and Clive right beside them, were in every scene. So much for the theory that the parents were trying to stop the children. It looked to me like they were just as involved as their offspring. In each of the scenes I noticed another figure, not a Neilson, hiding in the shadows. He—I had the feeling it was a he—didn't try to stop what was happening. He didn't try to help, either. I got the sense he was watching, waiting to report back to someone.

The other piece of the puzzle I needed to work through involved Lara. In the last flicker of my dream before I woke up, I saw Lara, in the city, talking to Margie Neilson. I didn't get the sense that Lara was doing anything wrong, but she was hiding something. She hadn't mentioned that she knew Margie. That concerned me.

I closed my eyes as I let the shower work its magic. Alternating between hot and cold water was a trick I used to clear away the brain fog and the cobwebs. I felt the excess energy from my dreams washing down the drain, along with the residue from the gathering last night. I stayed under the water a minute or so longer.

Green-brown eyes stared back at me as I gazed into the mirror. My long, brown hair mirrored my face, hanging limp and wet, as I brushed out the knots. Not one of my favourite things to do. Being able to look at myself in the mirror was a skill I'd yet to master. Looking at myself in the mirror without cringing would help remove self-doubt. I had read that in a book once, years ago, and it stuck with me. Today I was able to look into the mirror, and smile at the person looking back at me.

My gaze wandered around the bathroom. The crisp white paint with accents of baby blue. Tiles with a hint of blue lined the floor, continuing up the walls to just above my waist height. The modern shower cubicle fitted in the space that had once held a much older shower over bath set-up. Every room in the house was an example of my parents' hard work. I'd need to repaint in a few years, but the tiles, plumbing, lighting, sinks, and floorboards were either repaired or replaced within the last ten years.

For the first time in over a year I felt my energy, at the core of my being, lift. Like a heavy weight taken off a barbell I held. Butterflies in my stomach—I realised that instead of dread, I was looking forward to what the day was going to bring.

Chapter 12

Sunday was normally the day I cleaned the house, made my meals for the week, and tidied up the garden. "I'm giving myself the day off," I told Buddy, feeding him a carrot and half of my apple. I took my second cup of coffee to the wicker chairs and table which sat under an awning on the house side of the vegetable patch. The smell of basil and peppermint in the pots reminded me of many other days spent chilling outside in my parents' favourite place to unwind after a busy week at work. Seamus nearly always occupied the fourth seat unless I was at the farm with his family.

"Sunday is for relaxing and enjoying life. I'm slowly remembering that," I told Buddy as I opened the book I had started reading a week ago.

One hundred pages later I considered ignoring the flashing light on my mobile. Whoever was messaging me could wait until I read the remaining ninety-five pages.

"I haven't changed that much," I told Buddy who was nuzzling up near me, hoping for another morsel of food.

The tinkling of the latch on the side gate caught my attention. "You can't hide away young lady." Seamus handed me a takeaway cup and flopped down on the chair opposite me. The same chair he used to occupy most afternoons and for meals on weekends.

"I'm not hiding away. I was having a lazy Sunday morning. It was either this or clean the bathroom. And anyway, I wasn't ignoring you, I was about to reply to your text." I tucked my bookmark into the book, resigned that I would have to read the rest later, maybe tonight.

"In that case, the mocha is a reward for your metamorphosis. I was certain you'd be scrubbing up a storm or mopping the floors." He held the other mug up. "Mine's because its Sunday."

My best friend in the whole wide world, there was nothing I wouldn't tell Seamus, unless I was cranky with him. When this happened, he just patiently waited for me to calm down.

"There's more." I grinned. "My second sight's back. I saw the Neilsons at each of the incidents. All of them. The children and Clive and Margie. Someone else was watching them." I briefly considered if the person was someone I recognised. The energy of the figure appeared dark and selfish.

"It wasn't me," he said, with a chuckle.

"I know it wasn't you. I'd love to know who it is and what was motivating them, whether they were behind it, or just accidentally witnessing it all." I sipped my mocha, just the right mix of sweet and bitter. "You do know that's infuriating, that you can still read my mind, after all these years?" I stopped, contemplating my words. "Actually, sometimes it's useful," I admitted.

"I know." He grinned, ducking as I swiped at him with my book.

"Did you just call in to bring me a drink?" I asked.

"That, and I wanted to check in to see how you were feeling after last night. That was a big deal—meeting with Mrs Marigold, Agnes, and that you were so open about it at the table afterwards."

"About that. Can we trust Jon and Lara?" I asked. "We don't really know them."

Seamus looked at me, I could tell he was thinking about my question. I realised my empath abilities were returning. My ability to gauge how people were feeling, their emotions and their motives. I didn't have to tell Seamus. He would've already noticed.

"I think we can trust them. Although they're from the city, both seem committed to our town. Why do you ask? Do you think one or both have an ulterior motive?"

"Not really. I trust them too. I haven't had any sense of either of them hiding anything from us."

"But?"

"But, in my dream I saw Lara in the city, talking to Mrs Neilson. She hasn't mentioned it at all."

"Let's ask her next time we see her. I'm sure there's a reasonable explanation."

"Me too." We drank the rest of our drinks in silence.

Seamus' phone beeped. "We are being summoned, or rather invited to coffee at the café."

"Don't any of us eat at home anymore?" I asked. "Lara or Jon?"

"Both," he confirmed as another beep sounded. "I have my car, unless you want to walk?"

"Do you mind if I walk? It's all downhill. Can you order me a water and a juice? I didn't think it would happen, but I've consumed my fill of coffee this morning already."

"Sure, I'll let the others know you will be a few minutes. Depending on traffic, you might even beat me."

Spirit Town was its quietest on a Sunday morning. Traffic mostly consisted of little old ladies on their way to church, farmers picking up the paper and a pie from the bakery, or families off on a picnic. It was peaceful as I walked the five hundred metres to the café. I waved to a couple of the oldies on their way into church. I did note, in the distance little puffs of rainbow smoke, like fairy floss, floating up from a house near the river. Was Miss Bluebell baking cakes again? Our home economics teacher showed us a trick for cooking perfect cupcakes every time. Maybe one of her students was practicing for a test?

"We need frequent flyers points for the café, we've been here so often." Jon was speaking to Evie, as I slid into the seat next to Lara.

"I was thinking the same thing, buy four and get the fifth drink free, that sort of thing," Evie replied.

"I'd sign up for that," I agreed. "Muffins would be another good one. As in buy four and get the fifth one free."

"True," Evie said.

"I'm thinking of a similar promotion at my shop. I can mock up a customer card for you as well if you like," Lara said.

"That's awfully generous of you," Evie said. "Only if you let me pay."

"We can work out the details later. I'll bring a sample over during the week."

As Evie left the table to get our order, I told the others, "My second sight has returned. According to what I saw, the Neilsons are involved. There's someone else in town who knows what's going on. I couldn't tell if they were just watching or if they're responsible as well. If we can find that person, we may have an actual witness." I turned towards Lara. "I have to ask, do you know Margie Neilson, from the city?"

"Do I? I don't think so." Her forehead creased, her eyes looking down to the right as she thought about it. "Oh, hang on, she's Margie the hairdresser? Of course!" she smacked her forehead with her right hand. Jon handed her the photo of the Neilsons. "Yep, that's her. I didn't know her last name. She owned the hairdressers near where I worked in the city. When I told her I was moving here, she was interested. I thought it was just the gossipy, hairdresser vibe. I haven't seen her here since I moved here." Lara looked at me, the others. "You do believe me, don't you? My goodness, do you think I had anything to do with all this?"

I looked at Lara, then over to the others. "No, I don't really think you had anything to do with it. I saw you in my dream, talking to her. I needed to ask you about it. It was more about testing my accuracy."

Lara leant over and hugged me. I sensed the relief in her energy.

"From a police perspective, what's the next move? Assuming you need evidence, rather than supernatural hooey?" I asked Jon.

He smiled. "Evidence, a witness, and a motive would be good. We didn't get anywhere last time we visited Clive and Margie at their farm."

"Can I put an article in the paper?" I mused. "I mean I know I can,"—staring at Seamus, beating him to the punchline—"I own the paper. What I mean is, can I publish an appeal for information? Will it cause problems or upset anyone?"

"The folk last night supported our appeal for information. I think asking the public for further assistance is a good idea. What do you think Seamus?" Jon enquired.

"I agree. Most people are keen for the festival to go ahead. I'm sure Izzie will ask the same question on the radio if we ask her," Seamus suggested.

"I don't see this town as gifted people and non-gifted. Everyone's capable of making the choice, doing the right thing, or the wrong thing," Lara said quietly.

"Are you sure I can't tempt you with food?" Evie asked as she delivered four glasses of pineapple juice to the table.

"Not now, thanks Evie, but I'm sure we'll be back later today," Seamus said with a wink.

Jon's phone rang. He excused himself and walked to the door. His voice was muted as he turned away, I couldn't hear any of the conversation. "Let's hope that isn't about any new drama or event," I said aloud. The others nodded their agreement. .

"Fred was just updating me." Jon noticed our looks of concern as he returned to the table. "The cattle disappeared overnight. I'm assuming their owner took them back. Apart from increased foot traffic in the park thanks to the amazing garden George created there's nothing else to report. I'm going to take a drive out to the Neilson's place later. Just to have a sticky beak and see if there is anything odd."

"Can we all go?" Lara asked. "Not in the police car, but in mine or Seamus'? If I see Margie, I'd like to stop and say hi."

"I'm game if you are." Seamus and Jon nodded. They all looked at me expectantly, as a wave of exhaustion swept over me. I saw a group of youths at a farm, causing trouble, throwing rocks at cattle and people.

"I think we had better go now," I said. "I'll explain when we're in the car." Without a word we drank the rest of our juices and waved to Evie as we left.

"I didn't recognise the youths, but they're throwing rocks or clumps of mud at cattle and at people on a farm, near some sheds with farm machinery. Five youths I think there were," I told them as Seamus increased speed a little in his big ute. *Oversized, yank tank*, I called it. Every time I climbed into the front seat, it felt like climbing up into a truck. It was just as difficult to climb into the back with Lara. Jon took the front seat.

"Does this happen often? And is it only when there's trouble, or do you get second sight about the weather or a sale at the shops?" Lara asked. I sensed she was worried about what we would find at the farm. Distracting herself, asking questions.

"Good question. It depends on what's going on. It can be as simple as knowing I'm about to run into you, or there's a story I could follow for the paper. I know when friends or family are going to ring if I tune into the gift. I can tune in or out, but not always. Sometimes it seems it has a mind of its own."

"You were right this time," Jon said as Seamus stopped at the gate. A group of five teenagers were standing at the gate, laughing, and yelling across the fence. I could see the Neilsons in their shed, trying to ignore the commotion.

"Okay you lot, head home or I'll take your names and call your parents. Go on, now, I'm not joking about this, go!" There was no uncertainty or doubt in Jon's tone. If the youths doubted he was serious, the utility belt around his waist was a good deterrent as well. With a mouthful of swear words and kicking of the ground, the youths reluctantly got back into their mustang and drove off in a cloud of red farm dust.

Clive, Margie and their three children came out to the gate.

"Was that a coincidence, or does the law now know what's going to happen ahead of time?" Clive asked, sarcasm dripping from every word.

Seamus pointed to me. "Beth here has second sight, when it works," he said good naturedly, trying to lighten the mood. "She saw that there might have been some trouble out here so we all came for a drive to see if we could help out."

"I could say that we could have handled it ourselves," Clive said, "but instead I'll thank you for coming to help." I marvelled at how Seamus had the ability to diffuse a volatile situation. He had done so plenty of times growing up when I'd inadvertently said the wrong thing.

"Would you like to come in for a cup of tea?" Margie asked.

"That would be lovely thank you!" Lara said softly. "I think we met in the city, before we both moved here?"

Margie squinted at Lara. She raised her hand to the top of her head, her fingers moving around until she touched her glasses. She moved them down over her eyes and squinted again. "I recognise you now, Laura, isn't it? I remember you used to come in for a cut and style."

"Lara." She smiled. "Yes. I keep meaning to make an appointment in town, but there is so much to do when you move somewhere new. Getting the business established and settling into everything. It's taking me longer than I imagined. Can I help you make the cuppas?" As Clive opened the gate, Lara linked her arm in Margie's. Their heads tucked in together as if friends for years, they chatted as they led the way into the kitchen.

"I remember you from a long time ago. You were just a baby," Clive said. "I knew your parents." I smiled not knowing what to say. "I had a lot of respect for them," he continued. "They treated me and everyone else fairly, with respect. Special powers or not, we were all the same in their eyes."

"I'm still learning how to fill their shoes. I've made some progress, but I'm not there yet."

Their farmhouse kitchen was huge. The hub of the house with three teenagers, a big wooden table that would fit ten people took up the space in the middle. The earthy hues and the pale walls gave the room a comforting atmosphere. The big window at the sink, that ran the length of the wall, overlooked an outside covered area that led on to a trellised vegetable garden.

Margie placed two plates of muffins in the middle of the table. A bowl full of apples, oranges, bananas, kiwi fruit and passionfruit sat alongside it. I watched in awe as the children swooped in, grabbed some food and sat down at the huge park bench located just outside the kitchen, through sliding glass doors. I heard but couldn't make out the details as the teens teased each other; good natured bantering that I never understood. An only child, with no cousins, and as an adult with no children, I never figured out that sibling bond. Except for Seamus, that is. We had been inseparable for many years.

"Help yourselves to muffins, or fruit." Margie offered, as Lara handed us each a cup of tea.

As we sipped our teas, Seamus asked conversationally, "What made you guys return to Spirit Town? I heard you were home schooling your kids. If you are, you both deserve a medal."

Margie looked at Clive. "We both grew up in small towns and wanted our children to experience living in the country, instead of the city. Home schooling didn't work as well as we'd hoped. Kylie, Jim and Ted go to Spirit Town high school now. After school they work with us on the farm. We run cattle, in addition to the potatoes and pumpkins, which are relatively low maintenance crops."

I could see the kids outside, mucking about with a football. They looked and behaved the same as any other teenagers as far as I could tell. They all had Clive's ginger coloured hair and all three were taller than their parents. I wasn't sure what I had expected to see. No one was sitting sulking, or even playing with their mobile phones. The family dogs were running around, chasing the football. A black cat was ignoring the fuss, preening itself on the sideboard in the corner. Could I get any intuitive inkling about the children and their behaviour?

I wasn't used to focusing my second sight or intuition on any particular question. It felt like I was trying to force it. Their auras blended, creating a mix of colours that I couldn't distinguish as belonging to any individual. Emotions, too, were all over the place. Wasn't that normal for teenagers? I couldn't remember. Trying to pick up on anything specific was exhausting. I tuned back into the conversation in the room.

"Did you and the kids find it difficult moving from the city?" Lara asked.

This time Clive answered, "We all love the big open spaces now that we're at the farm. We love the feel of the small-town community. Getting to know everyone will take time, but overall, we're glad we made the move." I could tell Margie and Clive were both holding back. They were friendly, offering answers to our questions, but there was a hesitation there. As if there was something left unsaid.

Once we'd all finished our tea, I realised we weren't going to get any more information. "Thanks for the tea and muffins. I think it's time we left you to enjoy the rest of your Sunday." I didn't want to outstay our welcome. The others followed my cue.

"Maybe we can catch up for a coffee one day," Lara suggested to Margie.

The whole family joined their parents at their gate to wave goodbye. As I climbed into the back seat, a flash of orange light caught my attention. I turned to the Neilsons. Their auras were still entwined, but I could make out a mix of orange and green, with shades of brown in what appeared to be a protective layer around them. More than the auras I could see, I felt empathically, that the parents were protecting the teens; protecting and hiding something. The teens' energies were all over the place. I remembered Mr Moore's comments the previous evening that the awakening of our powers was more disrupting in this generation. I felt as if the young girl was trying to send me a message. Something about innocence and a wish to tell the truth.

I couldn't help smiling—my powers were back!

Chapter 13

"That went well," Jon said. "I'm being serious," he added.

After the visit to the Neilsons farm, I suggested we go for a walk. The shady canopy of trees in the bottom park was the perfect location. It was either that or reconvene for even more coffee. Not that we had ruled out heading to the café later.

"Yes, it did," Seamus agreed. "I mean they didn't confess to anything, but they didn't chase us off their farm with shot guns."

"Does that mean they took part in the incidents, or not? Did anyone get a feel for that? Seamus, Beth?" Lara asked, kicking off her shoes and wiggling her toes through the grass.

I followed her lead, taking my shoes off and allowing my feet to find the earth beneath them. A trick to find balance. Being grounded by mother earth. Feeling the soft, lush, cool blades of grass between my feet. "There didn't appear to be any malice or evil intent surrounding either Clive or Margie. The children's energy was all over the place. The parents are protecting them. The young girl wanted to tell us more. None of them mean any harm, but they played a part in each of the incidents. I don't think they had a choice. I get a sense of confusion and wanting to do the right thing, but not knowing who to trust. Seamus, how about you, what did you pick up on?"

"You know I can't read everyone's minds, right? For reasons unknown to me only a select few are chosen." Lara and Jon raised their eyebrows at his response, but neither asked the question I suspected they wanted to. "What I do pick up, every time we're near Clive and Margie, is that they feel stuck, as if they have no say in what's happening. Almost like there's a puppeteer pulling their strings, making them make the wrong choices."

I shivered.

"What's wrong?" Lara asked, "Are you cold? We can walk up in the top park, there is more sun there."

"As Seamus described what he picked up on, I saw an out of focus image of three people. They were facing away from me. The bigger one was well dressed and a little older than us. The other two were only young, similar ages to Margie and Clive's children. The feeling of selfishness and greed. The sort of feeling you get with a thief, a criminal of some kind. The lengths they go to for their own benefit."

"I don't suppose you could identify any of them?" Jon asked. I shook my head.

"Nope. I mean there's a sense of power with the older person. I get the feeling that we know them, but I can't work out who it is."

MONDAY STARTED THE same as Sunday. I woke up before dawn, capturing on paper as much as I could remember about my dreams. The figures in black, the men in business suits, characters in stripy suits and little stripy hats stealing things in big sacks slung over their shoulder. With no identifying marks or features I wasn't sure that this was a helpful clue. The sense of anger, greed and selfishness grew stronger. The emotions attached to the dream, the people who were behind the incidents. I suspected there was more trouble to come.

I looked out the window at where Buddy was grazing. Such a simple life. Grazing, looking at the garden, sleeping. I needed to remember to spend some time with him after work.

I hopped in the car, determined to get to work early and to focus. No distractions. *No coffee or muffins until the week's paper is planned.* I trusted and loved Lexi. She practically ran the place without me. She was competent, and she didn't really need my input. That being said, I love writing and organising, and Lexi was happy for me to manage the big stuff so she could concentrate on being creative. With the festival less than two weeks away, I felt the need to ensure everything was under control.

"I thought I was early." Lexi she rushed in, bringing in the positive energy of her youth. "Good morning. I brought muffins. Choc chip. I'll put the kettle on, and we can get started, unless of course you've already planned out the week." She grinned.

"Thanks Lexi. I hope you had a great weekend." I followed her to the kitchen and popped some peppermint tea bags into our cups.

"I always do!" Her smiled sparkled. "I heard there was some excitement while I was away. If I'd known we were going to have so much going on, I would've postponed the parental visit."

"Ah, but we can't see the future, can we?" I asked, then realising what I said, I amended it. "Well, generally we can't." Lexi knew a little about my gift, although we had never had a conversation about it. I put that on my list for later in the week. After years of pretending, like most of the townsfolk, that magic didn't exist, maybe it was time to call it out and speak openly about my gifts.

"A lot happened over the weekend." As we sat at the table in the conference room, I decided to share some of the adventures of the last two days. "The gates returned, undamaged and as good as new. Some cattle decided to come into town for a Saturday morning visit. They returned home as mysteriously as they arrived." I took a sip of my tea. "Jon doesn't have any strong leads, but he's following up on some things. We, Seamus, Jon, Lara, and I, met with Mrs Marigold and some of the people who meet at the old church. They couldn't provide any firm leads." I paused, taking a bite of one of the muffins. "These are delicious, thanks."

"What about if we ran an article, asking for people to come forward if they had any information?" Lexi suggested.

"Great minds think alike. I was thinking along the same lines, but I don't want that to be the focus of the edition. I mean, we want to know what is going on and why, and we want to resolve this before the festival. I'd like to continue that positive aspect we worked on last Friday. How about if we run an article where we list the many reasons why our festival benefits our town? It brings our town together, encourages tourists to visit ... I'm sure we could come up with ten points."

"Perfect." Lexi's eyes danced as she drew sketches with a stylus on her tablet, little diagrams about how she saw it could all fit together. I admired her drawing skills.

"If you work out how it will look on paper, I'll contact Izzie and Sharon and tell them our idea. I'm sure they'll be willing to run a similar campaign." I stood up, eyeing the plate which still held four muffins. Tempting, but I told myself that I could come back for another one after I finished my tasks.

I EMERGED FROM MY OFFICE an hour later. "I'm going for a walk, before I eat another of your delicious muffins," I told Lexi. "Izzie and Sharon are on board with our plans to promote the festival. I'm going to call into the health food store, to check with Lara that she's judging the window competition. In all the fuss of the last week, forgot to double check."

"Have fun." Lexi waved. She had a mock-up of our paper spread out on the table, plotting out the latest edition. She loved the physical aspects of putting the paper together, piece by piece. I preferred the computer programme, after years of the old ways. I loved the way our skills complimented each other.

"Good morning, Beth." I was greeted as I opened the front door of the newspaper office. "I was just calling in to see you."

"Good morning, Mrs Marigold," I replied.

"Call me Agnes, dear," she reminded me, "school was such a long time ago." She had a point. I still called teachers and friends of my parents 'Mr and Mrs'. Calling them by their first name seemed disrespectful. But if Mrs Marigold would like me to call her Agnes, then I would do my best to call her Agnes.

"Agnes," I repeated, with a tiny smile.

"That didn't hurt a bit, did it?" she said mischievously. "Are you going to invite me into your office? I have something I'd like to discuss with you, in private, if you have a few minutes."

"Of course, Agnes, come in." Lexi looked up as we walked past the meeting room. She smiled and nodded to Agnes as I led my visitor through the door to my office. "Would you like a cup of tea or coffee, or some water?" I offered.

"I'm fine dear, thanks for asking. I had a cup of dandelion tea before I left home. It'll keep me going for a few hours." I tried not to shudder at the thought of dandelion tea. Its bitter taste meant it was good for me, but still I only drank it rarely. "I won't keep you long, I know you're busy." As she sat down in the chair in front of my desk, she placed the basket she was holding on her lap. "I have a gift for you," she said, lifting the lid of the basket. Her hands held the most adorable, tiny ball of ginger and white fluff.

My heart melted. I absolutely love cats. I had been putting off getting another feline companion. My excuses included: the long hours I worked, I might want to go away for the weekend, I already had Buddy, I couldn't have another pet ... the list went on and on.

"I couldn't possibly accept such a generous gift," I said reluctantly, my whole body yearning, aching, to hold that little ball of fluff.

"Whether you think you're accepting him or not, I'm not leaving here with him. You can agree to look after him, or not. It has nothing to do with me," Agnes said briskly.

"I didn't mean to offend you," I responded. "I would love to look after him. I struggle with people being generous towards me."

"I could say *pot calling kettle,* but I won't. We both know how much you do for our town. Anyway, this isn't me being generous. He is your familiar. He appeared after your visit to our gathering. You're now open and accepting of the skills and abilities that you've been gifted with. I'm not saying we are witches, but you my dear, need a familiar to help and support you as you embrace your unique gifts." Agnes stood up and placed the bundle of fluff firmly in my hands on my lap.

"Spark," I said the word aloud. I couldn't stop it; it just came out. "That's his name. It could be flame, but he's not yet big enough. He's the little spark, the spark that starts it all and grows into some magnificent."

Agnes nodded. "I know. I know those words just materialised for you. That's Spark, your familiar working with you and through you. Your bond is strong already." She picked up her basket, linking it on her right arm. "I'm proud of you, Beth. I was waiting to see how long it would take you—for your intuition to override your stubbornness, and your sense of right and wrong. Those intellectual aspects that make you who you are. You couldn't see how you could be both extra ordinary and logical. I knew one day it would happen; I'm so glad it did."

I nodded, having no words to respond to those that Agnes had eloquently spoken. I struggled to find words, to speak. Plus, Spark was distracting me, tickling me as he kneaded my lap with his tiny paws, his purring soothing to my soul. "Thank you," I managed to get some words out, as Agnes quietly slipped away. I took a minute to compose myself. I was in awe of what just happened, but the implications of those words would have to wait until later.

I held Spark up so that we were face to face. I was definitely a cat person. His dainty little whiskers, deep blue eyes and adorable little nose sent shivers of joy throughout my body. "Hi little guy, Spark," I whispered to him. He reached out his tiny front paws and ever so softly mewed at me.

Clasping Spark gently and firmly to my chest, I walked out to where Lexi was punching the keys on her keyboard. Sparks whole body vibrated as he purred, snuggled into mine.

"Aww who's your new friend?" she asked, jumping up off her seat, reaching her hand out to stroke the fur of the tiny bundle of magic in my hands.

"This is Spark. Mrs Marigold—Agnes—just left him with me. I'm his new friend." Owner was definitely the wrong word for the relationship between this gorgeous little creature and myself. "Is that an empty paper box I spy under your desk? Can I use it as a bed for Spark until I arrange something more permanent for him?"

"Certainly!" Lexi handed me the box with one hand, rummaging in her desk cupboard with the other, "Ah ha here it is!" Lexi pulled out a pale apricot coloured cardigan. "This was in the cupboard when I started my job. That was a few years ago now, but every time I go to throw it away, a little voice tells me to keep it because I'll need it one day. It turns out this is the day. Spark will be able to snuggle up in that. Do you have a saucer and some milk? I know that sounds odd, but I have a saucer in here. Mum insists on sending me cup and saucer sets, but I only ever use the cups." She passed me a dainty saucer with yellow and red roses painted all over it. "There's fresh milk in the fridge. I brought it in this morning. Not that UHT stuff you drink. Proper milk."

"Thanks Lexi. Give me five minutes to set up a space for Spark, although he may just stay in my arms for a while. Then we can get the articles sorted."

"I can talk you through my idea while you set him up if you like." I nodded. Lexi followed me to the kitchenette and back to my office.

"The paper basically keeps the same format as always. All the regular columns, adverts, that sort of thing. Because it's less than two weeks before our festival, all the articles will focus on that event. Stories of highlights and winners from previous years. Then and now stories of some of the locals who have featured throughout the years. I've a couple of fun competitions people can enter to win prizes. We've a cupboard full of donations from local businesses, prizes for the festival competitions. In our article we can appeal for any information on the events of the last week.

"The festival magazine arrived from the printers. It includes all the times and dates for the parade, the fashion show, the boat race, the judging of the fruit, veg, cattle etc. I was thinking of including it in both editions this week and next week. We could order more copies if we need to."

"Perfect. You certainly sound like you have everything under control. Great work, Lexi." While she had been talking, I'd tucked the cardigan in the box and placed the box behind my desk. The milk was in the saucer, where I didn't think I would accidentally tread in it. Spark was still firmly in my arms with his eyes shut, purring loudly. "I have an article about the strange events of the last week. It's a tongue in cheek light piece asking if people think what happened was all just hype for the festival, with our wicked witch character as the perpetrator, or whether there's a criminal, underhand element to it all. I don't expect people to respond, but I'm curious to see if they do. I'll work on similar light heartened, *what if* articles for the next couple of editions too."

"Thanks, Beth. I'm loving this job." Lexi's energy was contagious.

"It feels like we've been doing this for years—we work well together." I was confident that she could independently run the whole thing. We made sure we had the editions planned out at least a month ahead. For big events, like the festival, Lexi was keen to make sure she didn't miss anything. We agreed the balance between planning ahead and responding to news and events as they happened was key to keeping the paper popular.

Reluctantly, I placed my sleeping kitten into his makeshift bed. I made myself a black coffee; my drink of choice at work when there were things to do. I thought about Agnes' words. My forehead tingled, indicating my third eye was working again. I was yet to master the skill of using my third eye; I found it tuned itself in and out, pulsing as it tuned into the people around me.

Agnes was right. I'd been so concerned about being *normal,* practical and using only my common sense, that I was doing a disservice to half the town. Not on purpose, but because I wasn't using my skills. I didn't want to be identified as different, but I was and I should have been proud of that. I could be both businesslike and logical, and supernatural. I didn't have to start wearing hippy pants or kaftans, belong to a coven, or dance naked in the full moon.

I suspected that even while he was asleep, Spark was sending me words and ideas. I caught myself smiling. Almost unheard of around here. I was the serious one. The businesslike, efficient one. Maybe I could be both.

Down to business, Beth, I whispered softly to myself. If I could respond to my outstanding emails and snail mail on my desk in record time, I would have more time to play with Spark.

"I'm just taking an early lunch to run some errands." Lexi popped her head around my room. "When I come back would you like me to mind Spark while you meet the others at the café?"

I frowned, puzzled. Did I have a meeting I forgot about? I couldn't remember planning to meet anyone.

Noting my confusion, Lexi clarified, "Oh sorry, I must have forgotten to tell you. Jon rang while Mrs Marigold was here. He wants to meet up with you, Lara, and Seamus at twelve- thirty."

I glanced at Spark. He was gazing up at me, quietly waiting and watching. I reached in and gently picked him up, cuddling him.

Such a tiny time waster, my dad would have called him. He much preferred dogs, but he had a soft spot for the cats Mum and I loved so much as well.

"Thank you, Lexi. I'd love to take him with me, but Evie might have something to say about a kitten in the café. If you don't mind, when you come back, you can be on kitten-duty while I meet them for lunch."

"I would love that! I'll be back soon." Lexi left, the jingle of the outer door signifying she had left the building. Satisfied that I'd completed enough admin work to justify spending time getting to know my familiar, I turned my attention from my laptop to my newest friend. Spark was not much bigger than my favourite coffee mug, the one with the cats on it. He may have been part Persian, his fur seemed longer than a normal shorthaired cat. The mix of white and ginger on his coat reminded me of a pet rabbit I had named Caramel when I was in primary school.

Spark stretched, and after a discerning look around the office, started cleaning himself. Licking his paws, and his hind legs, all while balanced on my lap. My black trousers were collecting tiny pieces of his fur. He was so adorable I didn't mind. The old Beth would have been trying to brush off the fur while Spark was still there. I was besotted.

As I let myself sink into the truth that I had a familiar. An image of a person in dark clothes, arguing with the Neilson children came into focus. I sensed the person was about the same age as the children. In quick succession, I saw the Neilson kids, stealing from the corner store, and starting another fire. The darkly clothed figure was in each of the scenes. I was mesmerised. The scene changed. Max was talking to the dark figure. Yelling, waving his hands around in the air. I got the impression that the other person was being bullied. In the next scene, Max was counting money, large amounts of bills piled up on his desk. Spark uncurled himself and climbed up until his nose was touching mine. I inhaled the new kitten smell. That last picture was the one I needed to put it all together.

The dream like state, feeling ever so safe and loved. I couldn't keep the smile from my face, even though the revelation was huge, and I should be contacting the others straight away. There was time. This bond with Spark was amazing.

"Aren't you two just so cute." Lexi appeared back at the door.

"That was quick," I said, breaking my gaze and arranging Spark back on my lap.

"I was nearly half an hour. I was worried I was going to be late. It's pension pay week, the oldies were lined up at the Post Office, waiting to pay their bills." A lot of the older population weren't comfortable using the internet to pay bills. Some didn't even have a computer or a mobile phone.

"That's okay. As you can see, I was a little distracted." I handed Spark to Lexi, giving him a tiny kiss on the top of his head as I did so. It was interesting that I didn't need to speak out loud to Spark, he and I communicated by thoughts.

"We'll be fine. I'll give him a tour of the office, the kitchen and my desk. Go eat, talk, have fun." Lexi waved me away, already gooing and gaaing at Spark.

"I know you two will have a great time. I've no idea how long I'll be, maybe an hour. I'll pick up some kitten food and little toys for him on the way back." My mind raced with all the things I needed to buy on the way home for my new housemate.

"No need to do that. I may have already ducked into the two-dollar shop and found him some things." Lexi grinned.

Chapter 14

The others were sitting at the booth, with four cups of coffee and four plates piled with burgers, chips and salad on the table in front of them. Monday lunchtime was busy in the café. The line for takeaway burgers and coffees was long, and there were a few people seated, fingers on the keys of their laptops while they waited for their meals.

"Finally, you arrive." Seamus looked at Lara. "Now can we eat?" he asked. Lara nodded.

"I didn't think I was that late," I said sitting down next to Jon.

"You aren't late," Seamus said between mouthfuls of food. "I was early, and hungry. So, I ordered for everyone."

"Thanks, Seamus. I can see that. I can see I'll have to go for an extra-long walk this afternoon, after eating all this. It looks amazing, though." I didn't realise how hungry I was until I smelt the food. Using my intuition and second sight did tend to give me an appetite. "I have news. My spidey senses have kicked in. I think I know what's going on." The others all leant in, eager to hear what I had to say. I took a sip of my coffee, ate a chip and a piece of lettuce. "There was a figure dressed in dark clothes bullying the Neilson kids. I watched the kids stealing from the corner store, and starting another fire. Then I saw the dark figure being yelled at by Max. Finally, Max was in his office counting huge piles of money." I picked up my burger, and watched their faces while I ate some lunch.

"Are you saying Max is behind what is happening? That he's getting paid to sabotage the festival?" Lara asked. "Did it look like the Neilsons were being threatened, coerced to do those things?"

"Yes. It felt like the Neilsons had no choice. They were being bullied and threatened by Max's henchman," I marvelled at the delicious combination of flavours. Could having a familiar have awakened my senses this dramatically?

"You said you saw a theft and another fire?" Seamus asked, taking out his phone.

"Yes. I'm hoping neither event has happened yet," I answered.

"Clive, it's Seamus. You and Margie need to pick your kids up from school, now. Meet me at the café as soon as you have them. I'll explain when you get here."

"Jon, you're quiet, are you all right?" Lara asked, concern in her voice.

"I was just thinking of something my predecessor said about Max. *Watch your back.* He didn't accuse Max of anything, but the rumour was that Max was taking bribes from some big corporation. We can't do anything about it. Unless we find proof."

"I'm hoping the Neilsons will be able to provide the proof, once we tell them what Beth saw," Seamus agreed. "Otherwise, we'll have to take more drastic measures."

"Such as?" Jon raised his eyebrows.

"No idea, it just sounded good." Seamus shrugged.

"That was quick," I said a few minutes later as the Neilsons walked in and sat down at the empty table next to ours.

"We were at the school picking up the kids, when you rang," Margie said. The kids and Clive were whispering together.

"You know what second sight means don't you?" I asked the teenagers. They nodded, looking away or at their parents. "It's okay, I promise," I continued. "I saw what was going to happen this afternoon—that you were being bullied. I know you had no choice. Someone was threatening you. I saw who's behind it and we want to help put a stop to it all."

Jon took his cue from me. "We won't be charging your family for any of the damage. If you committed the crimes because you feared for your life or because you were being threatened, it wasn't entirely your fault. Are you able to tell us who is threatening you?"

The oldest one, Ted, answered, "One of the kids in my year, Eddie. His older brother too. They told us we would all end up in goal if we didn't do what they said. The mayor would make sure we were all sent away to separate goals, for a long time."

Jim added, "We didn't want to do the wrong thing. We told our parents about it. They weren't sure who we could trust. Yesterday, after you came around, we wondered if maybe we could trust you."

I wanted to be back in my office, or at home, playing with my new friend. Instead, I walked up to the counter. "Can we please have some more coffees, six of them. And a big bowl of chips and three milkshakes."

"Sure, I'll bring over some cake as well. It looks like they need some cheering up."

"Thanks, Evie, you're the best."

"Are you willing to provide a written statement?" Jon asked.

Margie glanced at Clive and her kids, before addressing Jon directly, "Yes, we'll each provide a statement, telling you everything we know about what happened. We trust that you will keep us safe."

"Thank you," Jon responded humbly. "The best thing would be for you to go straight home and stay there. I'll come out and take your statements once I have the others in custody. For your safety, I'll send one of the other officers with you. Just in case. I don't expect any trouble though. People like Eddie and his brother tend to be good at scaring people, but they rarely hurt anyone." He pointed to Fred, who had come into the café a few minutes earlier. "I have known Fred for years. I trust him. Finish your drinks. I need to brief Fred and make some calls." He motioned to Fred to follow him outside.

"If you need any groceries or errands run, just let me know," Lara told Margie. "Nothing is too much trouble." She reached out and patted Margie's hand.

The energy in the café had changed. The Neilson's were calmer now. Their flight or fight response was under control and they felt safe. It must be a relief to know that they weren't alone, that we heard and understood what was going on. The few other customers still finishing their lunches were reading or chatting quietly. I hoped it wasn't the calm before the storm and that everything was going to be okay.

Evie came to the table with a cardboard box. "I have some muffins and other goodies I want to send home with you guys, if that's okay. I got a little carried away baking this morning and made twice as much as I needed." She addressed us all, rather than Clive and Margie. Such a kind gesture. Her actions reminded me again how wonderfully kind and welcoming our little town was.

"Thank you, Evie. You spoil us." Seamus jumped in, keeping the mood light as usual. "I could polish this lot off and still be back for dinner."

Jon returned with Fred, who he formally introduced around the table. "Hi everyone. I mightn't remember all your names, but I'll try," Fred said, shaking the hand of each of us seated at the table, even the younger ones. "Are we ready to go?" he asked Clive and Margie. Everyone stood up.

Seamus handed the box of goodies to Clive. "I'll check in later just to see if there are any goodies left." He winked at the kids. They smiled.

When Fred and the others left the café, Seamus, Jon, Lara, and I sat back down. Our friendly café owner bought us a jug of ginger ale and a plate of garlic bread. "Looks like you need it," she said, waving her hand *no* when both Jon and I tried to pay her. I really wanted to get back to Spark. He would be having a ball with Lexi fussing over him. My whole body missed the feel of his soft fur. It felt like hours since I'd left the office, in reality it was less than an hour.

"Myra and Jack are going to the Hill's house. Here's hoping that Eddie and his brother Harry are home and not out creating havoc on behalf of the mayor. I'm going to make a visit to Max's office," Jon sighed.

"I'm coming with you, whether you like it or not. I'll stay in the car if you prefer, but you aren't going alone," Seamus told him firmly.

"Thanks. I appreciate the support," Jon responded. Turning to me he asked, "If you get any sense of any of this not going well, can you let me know? Send Seamus a text. I want to make sure everyone is safe."

"Will do. Is there anything else you need Lara or I to do?"

"Not at the moment, but I'll keep you updated."

"Can you walk with me to check on the shop?" Lara asked me.

"Sure thing." We walked the fifty metres to the health food shop in silence.

Ann and Peter were busy rearranging the shelves. "We're having a display for the festival. The kids are planning it all, it will be a surprise, even for me. We aren't entering the competition, seeing as I'm judging the window displays, but I didn't want to miss having the chance to get into the spirit of the festival. Juliet didn't think there would be a problem if we made it clear that our display isn't part of the competition," Lara explained. Once she was happy that they were fine and didn't need her, Lara led me back outside.

"Mrs Marigold—Agnes—came to see me this morning. It was the strangest thing. She thanked me, for coming to town. She gave me a copy of a recipe book. She said it had been in her family for generations." As Lara was speaking, I felt goosebumps fly up and down my arms under my cardigan. An image of Agnes and Lara in an old farm kitchen, making jams and preserves. Was it second sight or an image confirming something else? Remembering that Lara had moved to Spirit Town to find her family, I decided to keep that one to myself for now. Another task for after the festival is over, helping Lara find her family, if she wanted help.

"That's interesting. She must have taken a liking to you. I can trump you though. Come and see what Agnes gave me."

I opened the door to the office for Lara to walk in first. She stopped, two steps in. "He is just the cutest thing," I heard the emotion in her voice. Stepping around her, I closed the door, to make sure that my little ball of fluff didn't accidentally escape into the big wide world. Spark was chasing the end of a ball of white twine that Lexi was wriggling. He pounced with his tiny paws.

"He's adorable, isn't he?" At the sound of my voice, Spark stopped what he was doing and ran over to my feet. I bent down and scooped him up. I felt all my senses quiver, being this close to my familiar.

"May I hold him, just for a minute?"

"Of course." I handed Spark to Lara, as much as I didn't want to let him go, even for a second. Spark snuggled and nudged Lara, causing more oohs and aahs from her and Lexi.

"You're going to bring him in every day, aren't you?" Lexi asked. "I mean he's too small to be left home alone. I'll mind him any time you need to leave or have meetings. I can still get my work done as well. I promise!" I couldn't help smiling at Lexi's enthusiasm.

I pretended to think about my response. The truth is, I was planning on bringing Spark with me everywhere I could. I couldn't bear the thought of leaving him alone in the house for such a big part of each day. "I think so," I teased her, "if you think he won't distract us too much."

"If you're ever both too busy, I can help out too," Lara added, as Spark batted her with his paws. purring as he did so.

I laughed. "Okay, well I can see he has two very capable nannies. I'm going to make a couple of calls." I only got two steps towards my desk before my mobile rang. "It's Jon," I told Lara, as I pressed the green button. Lexi looked at us both. I could tell she was curious, but she didn't want to pry.

"Lexi, there's a lot I have to explain to you." I turned to Lara. "I trust Lexi." Lara nodded her approval.

"What I say here goes no further for now. Lexi, when we can print it, you can write the article. Brief version is that Max seems to be behind all the recent incidents. He coerced a couple of youths to bully some other youths into causing most of the damage over the last week." Addressing Lara I continued, "Max wasn't in his office. He's gone, so are all his papers, his personal effects, everything. The same at his house. It looks like he left in a hurry. He must've prepared an escape plan in case we discovered his criminal activities. The good news is that the Jack and Myra managed to find Eddie and Harry. They weren't home but their mum told the officers where they could be found. Their mother was very chatty. She and the mayor had been friends for years. Her boys thought of him as some kind of father figure. However, all three are more than happy to tell all they know about Max and his less than lawful behaviour. Jon and Seamus are heading out to the Neilsons now."

"Gosh. At least it sounds like everyone is safe." Lara stopped as her phone beeped. "Seamus, asking if I can meet them there, moral support for Margie." She patted Spark lovingly. "See you later, little fella. I suspect it'll be dinner at the café, again."

"One of us really should learn how to cook dinners for us all, but having someone else make the mess and clean-up is certainly worth paying good money for. Now go, and catch me up later." Once Lara had left, I turned back to Lexi. "If you'd like to make us a cup of peppermint tea each, and come into my office, I'll answer any questions you have." I could have made the cups myself but this way I got a couple of minutes to snuggle with my new bestie.

It was after four in the afternoon by the time Lexi and I finished talking through the events of the last week. Spark shared his time evenly between us both, before falling asleep in the crook of my arm.

"Do you think there is anyone else involved?" Lexi stood up and stretched her arms high above her head. "I mean, was it just Max or does the corruption reach further into our council and our business community?"

"I honestly don't know. Remember, it's only in the last day or so that my second sight has come back and it's only today that it revealed Max. Why, have you heard any gossip along those lines?"

"Not really, I mean there's always gossip and nonsense about people around town. I have a family dinner tonight for Mum's birthday. I'll keep my ears open. My family are always up for a gossip. I won't tell anyone anything about this though." She looked stricken, realising she had just said her family were gossips.

"I know you won't, Lexi. Otherwise, I wouldn't have told you. Go and have fun with your family. It's been a long day and its only Monday! I get the feeling it's going to be a big week." If Spark hadn't been asleep, I'd have handed him to Lexi for a cuddle. Instead, when she left I placed him in his box bed. Going by the time on my laptop, there was still time to make some business calls.

MY FIRST CALL WAS TO the deputy mayor, Ross Mac. I'd known Ross for over twenty years. We played tennis together for years, before he injured his knee and retired from the game. He answered on the first ring. "Hi, Beth. No, I don't know where Max is, before you ask."

"Ross, hi, I'm guessing I wouldn't be the first person to ask you that today," I ventured.

"Not even close. I wasn't prepared for the police to ask me that question. I'm used to Max not being in the office. He tends to disappear for days. *Off to the city for a terribly important appointment* he'd mutter, if pressed. This time it looks like he's gone for good. His office is empty, he's packed up and taken all his personal possessions, as well as all his documents, papers—the entire contents of his filing cabinet."

"I must ask, and don't take this the wrong way, but do you know what he's been up to? I don't think you were a part of any of it. I'm just curious if you had any inkling?"

"Of what, exactly? I thought he was just incompetent; abandoning his duties to spend time in the city with a woman. If Max's disappearing act is anything other than that I'm in the dark." After a few seconds Ross added, "Noting the amount of interest in his whereabouts today I'm guessing it's a whole lot more significant than I thought."

"Your guess is correct. I have two more questions. Did anyone unusual or unexpected ever visit his office that you were aware of? Dodgy, criminal types? I know the police will probably ask this."

"I honestly couldn't tell you. I was too busy focusing on my work and picking up the slack, the work Max was supposed to do. I didn't like the man and tried to not get involved in his business, unless I had to. You said you had two questions. What was the other?"

"How do you feel about stepping in as mayor? At least until after the festival and possibly longer?"

"I'd only step in on a temporary basis; I'm not interested in the role long term. I only took on this as no one else was interested the last time they called for nominations. I'm done. I'll help until we can find someone else, then I'm going back to my real job." Ross's real job was a combination of stone masonry and training horses. His stonework could be found on many of the farms and parks in ours and the surrounding towns. I understood he felt an obligation to step in the gap left when no one offered to take the role. Ross's father had been mayor years ago and had instilled a sense of community spirit in his son.

"Your father would be proud," I told him. "With regards to Max's behaviour and possible whereabouts, it's likely Jon will be in contact, if he hasn't already been. I'm chairing the festival committee meeting tomorrow night. Can you come along? I think you being there would boost the morale of the other members."

"I'll be there. It's one of the better parts of the job. Listen, I know the paper has already gone to print, so are you okay if I go on the radio tomorrow morning, informally announcing the mayor is indisposed and I'll be stepping in the interim? I want to get ahead of it before it becomes an issue. I can clarify that it's only temporary, until we can call an out of session, early election. It won't stop the gossips, but it takes away some of the mystery. We have enough of that at the moment."

"My thoughts exactly. I was going to ask if you were up for talking to Izzie on the radio in the next day or so. I'll follow up with an article with the same information in our next edition. Thanks, Ross. My next call will be to Izzie. I'll tell her to expect your call. My reason for ringing her is festival related, but it makes sense just to forewarn her a little, if you don't mind me giving her a summary of where we're up to."

I could hear the relief in Ross's voice. "Thanks, Beth, it saves me having that conversation with Izzie. I can just present her with the facts—Max is out of office; I'm stepping in until we find a permanent solution. I'm exhausted just thinking about the conversations I'm going to have to have in the next week. Let's catch up for a cuppa soon."

"Definitely. How is tomorrow morning, here in my office whenever you can get away?"

It was good to hear Ross chuckle. "Good old Beth, always on the ball. It's a date." I smiled, Ross was as energetic as I was, the only difference was he had never learnt the art of blocking negative energy. His slight build made it easy for people with negative energy to drain him, knowingly or unknowingly. Spark stirred and rolled over, but he didn't wake up.

My next call didn't start the way I had expected. Izzie recognised my number and didn't waste time on small talk "So it's true that our mayor's a criminal and that you chased him out of town?"

"No. Well, no to the second part of that question. The first part of your question I can't confirm or deny but you're definitely on the right track. Not that I told you that of course. That's only partly the reason why I rang. First things first—festival ads—can we talk about the festival on the radio every day from now until the event? Short slots of time, showcasing some different aspects." Pressing send on an email I drafted earlier, I continued, "I just sent you an email with what I propose."

"Yes, got it. That all looks okay. To be honest I hoped you would call about this. I want to make sure we put a positive slant on all this rubbish." A local, Izzie loved our town as much as I did. Leaving for a few years to study and work on her career, she too had returned to town, initially to care for her aging mother. She stayed, citing the relative peace and quiet of the smaller town as better for her mental health.

"Why don't you come around for a cuppa before work in the morning? You know where I live. Before you ask, yes, five in the morning is fine. I want to give you all the info, but I don't want to go into details on the phone. What I tell you, most of it you won't be able to divulge now. I'll answer all your questions as best I can. Lastly, Ross Mac will be in contact to ask to go on air tomorrow morning to confirm he has agreed to be interim mayor until we can find a more permanent solution. Max has left town."

"I'm intrigued and looking forward to catching up tomorrow morning. We don't do that often enough these days," Izzie replied. She and I were friends in high school and had met again at university, keeping in contact when Izzie moved back a few years ago. For all our promises to spend some quality time together, we were so career focused we rarely found the time.

"Thanks Izzie, I'm looking forward to catching up. I have a few more calls to make, but I'll see you bright and early tomorrow." Hanging up the phone, I checked my emails, reading message I had received from Juliet earlier in the day.

I'm unavailable to attend any further festival committee commitments.

Uncharacteristically for Juliet, there was no apology or explanation. In the few years I had worked with her, she was timid and apologetic, but she knew the council rules and regulations, which was handy. I briefly wondered if she and Max were in a relationship. I made a note to learn more about Juliet. Later. My list of things to do later was growing steadily today.

Spark stirred, so instead of ringing each of the festival committee members, I sent a group text.

Meeting Tues night. Usual place, 5.30pm.

I placed Spark on my desk nest to my laptop. I wasn't planning on getting into the habit of letting him jump up on the desk, but I wanted to watch and see what he'd do. He looked at me, seeking permission to explore. Gingerly placing his dainty little feet as he walked around, sniffing my phone and my laptop. I moved my mug when it looked like he was going to chase the dangly bit of the tea bag. My mobile beeped, startling Spark who jumped across it right into my lap. Luckily, I caught him in time. He tucked himself into a ball, kneading my lap and snuggled in. I added to my list—*send Agnes a basket of flowers, no, pots of fresh herbs as a thank you.*

A message from Lara *café.*

I responded, *yes, I'll be there soon.*

"What am I going to do with you?" I asked Spark, not wanting to leave him alone. Another beep.

This time the message was from Lexi, it simply said, *check the kitchen.*

I carried Spark with me. In the kitchen sat a washing basket. Inside it were packed several kitten sized blankets, a tray with a bag of kitty litter, kitten milk and food and some toys. Next to it sat a kitten carry case.

Wow thank you. I texted back.

"Problem solved," I told Spark as I placed him in the carry case. Thankful I had decided to drive this morning, I placed the basket and the carry case at the front door. Packing up my laptop and my phone from my desk I quickly turned off the lights, locked up and loaded up the car.

"I figure you will be safe in here," I said, patting Spark through the top of the carrier and making sure it was zipped up tightly. "I'll try not to be too long,"

Chapter 15

The café's *half price adult meal when purchasing a children's meal* on a Monday afternoon brought in a lot of families who wanted a night off from preparing dinner. I spotted the gang in the back booth, near the swinging door to the kitchen. It was far enough away from the nearest table that we wouldn't be overheard. The two young people who were serving the meals wouldn't be listening in to a group of middle-aged people chatting over pizza and garlic bread.

"I didn't know that Evie served at least three meals a day to those who couldn't normally afford to eat out," Jon was saying as I slid into the seat next to Lara.

"Monday nights she helps out at the homeless shelter, so we have young Kate and Emma serving the meals," Seamus explained. "Her parents are in the kitchen preparing the food."

"If we keep eating here, I'll have to join a gym," I said, half-seriously, half-jokingly. "I like not having to cook or clean up, so I appreciate when someone else organises all that for me. What did I miss?" I asked, tucking into a piece of garlic bread.

Seamus put down the piece of pizza, to fill me in of the details, before picking up the garlic bread and taking a massive bite. "The Neilsons have given us their statements. The kids told their parents that they were being bullied, forced to steal the gates, destroy the park, start the fires and the other incidents. Because there were prior incidents on record, Clive and Margie weren't sure what to do. They were scared that if they went to the police, their children would end up in jail. They were willing to take the blame if necessary. Thankfully, Jon was able to confirm that none of them will have to go to gaol.

The whole family want to undertake some community service, to make amends. They're going to start by helping at the festival, wherever we need them."

"Which is perfect," Lara piped up. "The more volunteers the better. I was thinking ushers or welcoming people to the various events. We can work out the details tomorrow afternoon."

Seamus picked up his story. "We found Eddie and his brother, Harry. They were very quick to blame Max. He paid them well to bully the others into committing the crimes. They chose the Neilsen's so the blame would rest with the gifted community. The Hill brothers admitted to being jealous of the unusual powers of their peers and were happy to help Max cause trouble. Neither of them was keen to end up in prison. They'll be assisting at the festival too. On clean up and garbage duty. Although they didn't volunteer themselves," he ended dryly.

"Max has provided more elusive," Jon said, taking up the tale. "No one's seen him for days. I have someone trying to track his phone, but it appears he's disabled that and his computer. We have officers in the city searching for his car."

I provided my update to the group. "I've spoken to Ross, and he's agreed to step in as interim Mayor. He doesn't know where Max is, but he isn't surprised that it's gone this way. He suspects Max is working with someone in the city, but he doesn't know any details. I trust him. I've known Ross for years. I spoke to Izzie, I'm briefing her properly in the morning, in person, not over the phone. She won't report the story until we say so."

"What's our next move?" Lara asked.

"We have the additional resources until after the festival. This is corporate crime as well as vandalism and public mischief. There will be additional patrols in case Max has organised any more trouble," Jon said. "I'm going to brief my boss soon, so I'm off to the station. I'll update you all when I have more information." Jon stood up, taking the last piece of pizza. "If no one else is going to."

"Do you guys want anything else?" Bessie asked on her way to the kitchen with a pile of empty plates in her arms.

"I think we're good, thanks so much for asking," Lara responded, at the same time as Seamus asked, "Do you have any cake and ice cream?"

"I'm going to pass on the dessert." I smiled at Bessie and the others. "But what about we meet here for coffee in the morning around seven thirty?"

"Give Spark a big cuddle for me." Lara said.. I left Lara to explain to Seamus, who Spark was and why I would be cuddling him.

Spark was sound asleep when I hopped in the car. Once we were home, he woke full of energy. He bounded around, exploring his new home. I made a cup of chamomile tea and watched my new friend. My familiar. It still blew my mind to think that in a couple of days so much had changed.

Spark padded over and started batting my feet with his front paws. I lifted him up to my lap. With his dainty feet tickling my skin, he climbed up the front of my shirt and on to my neck. I was surprised his claws didn't hurt or tear my skin.

"Hey there, little guy," I crooned. "I think it's bedtime. I'm tired; it's been a big day." Spark snuggled into my neck. I took that as agreement. Less than ten minutes later we were cuddled together, his purring lulling me into a deep and peaceful sleep.

I WOKE TO SPARK LICKING my cheek. "So, you're real; it wasn't a dream. The best alarm clock ever." The time on my phone said four thirty am. I placed Spark in his carrier and jumped in the shower. Dressed and ready for the day with the kettle boiling by ten to five. I opened the carrier so Spark could explore the kitchen. He lapped up some of the milk in the cute little saucer I found at the back of the shelf where I kept the good cups for when company came over.

I answered the door before Izzie could knock twice.

She enveloped me in a big hug. "Hello! Whoa, who is this little fella?" Spark was running in funny little hops between our feet.

"Izzie, meet Spark. He arrived yesterday and he is adorable."

"He sure is." Izzie was a dog person. I was a cat person. When we were twelve, Izzie spent most of her time trying to convince her mum to let her have a pony, a donkey, a lamb, and a monkey. Grown-up Izzie owned a terrier dog called Lucky, a big collection of books about animals, and an array of tiny china animals.

As we walked the few steps to the kitchen, I saw a flash of something. The image was too quick, and I was distracted. I dismissed it as a trick of the light.

Izzie perched on a kitchen chair, laptop still closed in her bag, holding Spark as he tried to chase her long, blonde curls. Giggling like little girls, we watched enthralled. The whistling kettle distracted us and Spark, who leapt out of her arms, bounding after the source of the noise. "Strong black," I said, placing the mug with horses in front of my friend.

"You remembered. Oh, and you kept this mug all these years." We had bought four mugs together. Izzie had kept the birds and dogs, I the cats and horses.

"I'm older, but not senile yet," I quipped. "While you drink your tea, let me tell you a story that you have to keep close to your chest until after the festival. I'll send you an email with all the details that I have as soon as I get into the office." Spark nudged my right foot. I picked him up and told Izzie the tale of the corrupt and evil mayor.

As I was speaking another image came to me. An empty block with excavators and machinery where a little row of shops should be. Storing the information away, I continued filling in on recent events, ending with the words, "That's as much as I know, so far. I'm sure there will be more."

"That's quite a story. I only have one question. As you were telling it, a strange look flickered on your face, just for a few seconds. What was that all about?" Izzie asked.

"Oh that. My second sight has come back, properly. That's how we got the breakthrough in the case. I wasn't going to tell you, only because I don't want you to think we solved the case because of my skills."

"But if you solved it because you put the pieces together, then well done you! Can I ask what you saw, just then?"

"You could ask, but I'm not sure yet. I'll have to go back to it and figure that out. Now, do you want another cuppa?"

"I'd love to, but I have to get to work. Let's catch up again soon and thank you for trusting me and telling me this story. I appreciate it and I can deflect any rumours, at least until after the festivities. Bye, little Spark," she whispered to the little ball of cuddles attempting to balance on my shoulders.

With some time to spare before meeting the others at the café, I carried Spark outside, holding him so he didn't jump down. "Hi, Buddy, this is Spark, your new little brother." The animals smelt each other. I kept a firm hold on the newest family member, just in case. I led Buddy into one of the other mini paddock areas, so he had fresh grass and weeds to munch on. His water bowl, a porcelain bath, contained enough fresh water from the light rain overnight. I wanted to bring Spark outside on a lead, probably on the weekend. Having tried half-heartedly with a previous cat, I wanted to give it a proper go this time. I had the feeling Spark would be a quick study.

After a few minutes of sibling bonding, I patted Buddy, knowing that with the committee meeting I would be home late again this evening. I made myself another cup, this time peppermint tea. Spark roamed the kitchen; I watched as he tiptoed out the door along the hall for a couple of steps. He turned around and bounded right back to my feet. He did the same through the door to my little library. The doors to the other rooms were closed. With no other dangers for a small kitten, I kept an eye on him as I sat and sipped my tea. I pondered what my second sight had shown me.

The vacant block was currently a row of five shops.

The seamstress in shop one—a business that belonged to my mother, which I now owned and managed. The three ladies who repaired and altered clothes and provided ironing services pretty much ran the place themselves. I'd not inherited my mums love of sewing, or clothing in general. I knew what looked nice and businesslike and I always made an effort, but I didn't have the patience to sew, mend or alter any item of clothing.

The twenty-four seven convenience store, which actually only opened until midnight and reopened at five each morning, was owned by relative newcomers to the town. They worked hard to ensure a variety of groceries available for their customers. The laundrette next door to the convenience store began as another of Mum's projects. She and a friend had started it to provide employment to some young friends and a place for people who didn't own a washing machine or dryer. Mum's friend, Heather, had no children so the business had passed to me. As with the seamstress, I managed things like building maintenance, repairs or improvements and upgrades, but pretty much let it run itself. The pay system for both stores were automated. I did monitor the takings, and the staff all knew to contact me if they needed anything.

The greengrocers always did well. People stopped on the way home for fresh vegetables for dinner. Run by a group of local farmers who sold their fresh produce, they sourced other vegetables and fruit from the markets in the city. The last shop in the row had been Dad's. A place for the men who loved woodwork to sell their creations. It was easier than having to lug their woodwork to the local markets all weekend. They volunteered their time in the shop. It pretty much managed itself, but with the understanding they could come to me about anything of concern.

Now I was concerned. The image that flashed in front of me was a building site where the row of shops had been. In addition to the excavator and machinery, I saw people in hard hats, workmen looking at plans. An uneasy feeling started as a dull ache in my stomach. Spark came over, stretching on his hind legs, trying to crawl up my leg. I scooped him up, burying my face in his fur.

"Did I miss a letter or an email about rezoning, or a problem with the building?" I asked him. "Is this part of what was Max up to?" Spark tapped me on the cheek with his paw. "If this is part of Max's plan, is he working with someone? Is there some conglomerate of businessmen in the city, trying to get the land and build some big shopping centre or hotel complex or something?" Another tap on my left cheek. "The first place to look would be the council. Things like that need planning permission. If Ross didn't mention anything, either it isn't a problem, or Max somehow passed this all through without going through the necessary channels." Another pat on the cheek. My stomach flipflopped. I had an uneasy, queasy feeling. It was only seven, thirty minutes before I was due to meet the others. "Let's go for a drive." I popped Spark into his carrier, picked up his bag of goodies and mine, and headed for the car.

I breathed a sigh of relief. The row of shops looked the same as they had always looked. Not a piece of machinery in site. "I think this means I have time to investigate and stop whatever plans Max has in motion, fingers crossed," I told Spark, who answered by purring loudly from the back seat.

This time, I arrived at the café before the others. I made sure Spark was comfortable and had a toy to keep him occupied. The café was bustling with its early morning energy. I spotted Greg in line and joined in behind him.

"Hi Greg, early start?"

"This is late for us. We're finishing up some construction work that has to be completed before the festival. Apparently, the mayor has some bug hush

hush project we're starting in a week. Everything else must be finished before that. Drama as usual when it comes to Max." Greg grinned.

"You've got that right," I said. "So, why's it hush hush, the new project?" I asked innocently. I hoped I was hiding the anxiety causing the churning in my stomach at the mention of a secret project of the mayors.

"Who knows?" He shrugged. "The word is he passed some dodgy project through a closed session of council a few weeks ago. It was rushed and without proper process or due diligence. I just hope it doesn't adversely impact the town. We have to do the job we're told to do, or we get sacked. Max made that very clear."

"I'm sure everyone will understand that you're just doing your job," I said reassuringly. I'd rather not have a job than work on a project that I suspected wasn't entirely legal or ethical. I did appreciate that the council workers, like Greg, who had a family to feed, couldn't necessarily be as picky when it came to paid employment.

Greg nodded. "I hope so."

Beth, my goodness, you look deep in thought for early Tuesday morning." Evie broke through my thoughts. "Is everything all right?"

"I'm sure it will be. I just have a busy day ahead. Can I order four mochas and two serves of raisin toast and a plate of fresh fruit, any fruit you have is fine." I knew she made a point of having healthy options available, should customers choose. "While I think of it, have you heard any rumours of new businesses being built around town?"

"Hmm, not really, there's always talk of a huge complex going in over the other side of town. It comes up every now and then. Why, do you know some juicy gossip?"

I smiled. "Not really, I just have this puzzle I am trying to solve."

"If you ask me, look at Max. He's dodgy. I know that's gossip, but he makes my skin crawl. I haven't seen him for a few days now, which is unusual. Maybe he's off with his fancy woman in the city."

"Maybe," I agreed. "Thanks Evie,"

I found Jon at what was becoming our regular table. "Morning, Lara is out tapping on the window of your car, I assume you have an animal in there," he said with a grin.

"My new kitten. Spark. He was given to me yesterday by Agnes Marigold, of all people." I sat in the seat across from Jon. Seamus and Lara sat down a few seconds later.

"Cute kitten," Seamus said as he and Lara joined the table. He knew how much I loved cats.

"How did Spark settle in last night?" Lara asked. "He's so cute."

"He's such an easy pet. No problems at all. I think we do have another problem though." I shared my vision and my theory of what it was all about. "With the planning for the festival I haven't been keeping up to date with council happenings. The shops pretty much run independently; I need to pay a long overdue visit to the shops this morning in case there's something I've missed."

No one spoke for a few seconds, each thinking about what I'd just told them.

"Surely not even Max would do that." Seamus shook his head. My dearest friend gave everyone the benefit of the doubt.

"If there was enough money in it, he would," I retorted. "I think he thought he could have convinced everyone he was the saviour of the town. If the festival failed due to vandalism and crime. The mayor jumps in with new business and employment opportunities for struggling townsfolk, that sort of thing."

"When you put it that way," Seamus mused. "And if he did, I will personally find him and make sure he pays for it; put him in jail for years."

I wasn't quite sure how to respond to Seamus's comment. He did tend to jump in to help the underdog. Years ago, he jumped in to defend me when I was too stubborn to back down. We were in our second year of high school, and our special powers were beginning to develop. The popular kids decided it would be fun to fill the teachers' cars with lemonade and marshmallows. I thought it was silly and tried to stop them. Maree and Linda challenged me to a magic duel. They were a few months older than me. I had no idea how to use my magic to duel, but I stood my ground. Seamus managed to calm the situation. His dad put on a weekend at the farm where we could all experiment with our magic. I loved him for stepping in and diffusing the incident, but I had yelled at him, telling him I could look after myself. It was a wonder we had remained friends.

Lara spoke quietly, "What's the plan? How can we help? Jon, you said you have the criminal part under control."

Jon nodded.

"I don't know yet. When I leave here, I'm going to call into the shops and talk to the other owners and managers to make sure we haven't missed some important piece of information. I want to know if they've heard any rumours, or if Max has visited there recently. Then I'll swing past Ross's office and see if he knows anything. I am sure he'd have told me if he did."

"Thanks, Evie," Lara said as Evie placed the mochas, raisin toast and fresh melons and grapes on the table in front of us. She'd added a bowl of tinned peaches and pears as well as individual plates for each of us to serve ourselves.

'Are we eating healthy today?" Seamus said eyeing the fruit and the raisin toast.

"Not really. I ordered us mocha, not green tea." I spooned some fruit into my bowl. My stomach was still aching and my shoulder twitched, the muscles tightening, although I was trying not to worry about the Wynyard shops.

"When I get into the shop, I'll see if my customers have heard any rumours. Today is the flash sale, twenty per cent off everything, so I'll be tied up in the shop all day. It means the chance to quietly interrogate everyone." Lara scooped some fruit into her bowl. "Thanks for the relatively healthy breakfast. I'll need energy for the day ahead."

"Most of our local shop owners have gotten on board with Lara's initiative; flash sales, two-for-one deals and other bargains to encourage locals to shop local." I filled Jon in. "We have shoppers visit from neighbouring towns to take advantage of the deals. The newspaper and the radio station actively support the local business community, providing free advertising space for promoting local business initiatives. Businesses showed their appreciation by taking out paid ads when they could.

I refrained from telling Jon the whole story. Long ago, one of the towns folk wove a spell that drew people into town to spend their money. On a windy autumn day, when the wind blew in a certain direction, you could still see the spell; a row of sparkly stars, wafting in the atmosphere. No harm done. Only people who were going to spend money anyway were affected, drawn to spend in our village.

"I have to spend some time at work today, too." Seamus sighed. "Luckily, I can get my fill of chatting to the customers. Tomorrow it'll be farm visits to see how it's all tracking. I get sidetracked so easily."

"We'd never have figured that out ourselves," I quipped.

"Uh oh, here comes trouble." For some reason, Seamus and Ross did not get on as well as I'd have liked. Izzie used to tease me they were both vying for my attention. A theory I quickly dismissed. I was friends with both, and that was how it was going to stay.

Ross ignored Seamus' comment and nodded his hello to the others at the table. "Beth, I'm so glad I caught you; Lexi said you would probably be here. I received the oddest call this morning about a demolition and construction order. The site where your parents' shops are located. I can't find any record of it in the council meeting notes or anywhere where it should be notated. I told the contractors to stop all work until they hear from me. I made it clear that any orders from Max are placed on hold. They weren't too pleased. Apparently, it was a big job. I'll try to get to the bottom of it."

"Have a seat. You look flustered. I'll order you a cuppa." I caught Evie's eye. "I only worked it out a few hours ago myself." He tilted his head a little to the right, a sign he was puzzled by my words. "Second sight," I reminded him.

"I must get to the station. I want to catch Max as soon as. I'll update you with news." Jon stood up. Lara and Seamus joined him.

"For something different, let's meet at the park for a late lunch catch up, at two. I'll bring the sandwiches and the drinks," I said firmly enough that the others didn't argue.

As they said their goodbyes and left the café I turned back to Ross. "Thank you, for figuring it out and putting a stop to the demolition and construction. I was going to visit you at your office when I left here to see if you could find any evidence of what I saw this morning." I took a breath, my heart beating erratically at the thought of losing the businesses my parents had worked so hard for.

"I' m just glad I found out about the proposal in enough time to stop the project. I have called an out of session council meeting for nine am this morning. I've my doubts about a couple of the other councillors. I'll make my position clear and inform them that the police are investigating. Anyone found guilty of working with Max will be held accountable and probably spend time behind bars." Ross looked at his watch. "I'd better go and prepare. I'll speak to Izzie afterwards."

"She's expecting your call." I stood up. I was keen to check on Spark, and get to the shops, after calling into the office to see Lexi.

"Typical Beth. Maybe you should be mayor," Ross said hopefully. "You certainly seem to have the energy, the determination and the networking skills for it."

"I think I have more than enough on my plate. Three, no four, businesses to manage is my limit. Unless you know of a way to give me more hours in a day." I waved to Evie as we left. Ross headed back to the council chambers; I hopped in my car to drive the short distance to my office.

"Ah, there's my little gorgeous friend, and hello to you too." Lexi took the carrier from my hand.

I placed the other bag of Spark's bits and pieces next to the carrier. "Hi Lexi. You know how you said you'd look after Spark anytime I needed you to?"

"Of course! Everything is under control here. You haven't got any calls, apart from Ross, but I'm assuming he caught up with you. Spark and I will have a wonderful time."

"Thanks Lexi. I'll be at the shops on Wynyard Street for an hour or so. Let me know if anything comes up." Spark patted me on my left cheek as I kissed him goodbye.

Chapter 16

It had been a few weeks since I had visited the shops in Wynyard Street. Excitement and anticipation still accompanied every visit to the place where my parents put in so much time and effort. They were humble people who wanted to provide opportunities for others in the community. I wasn't sure where their inheritance came from, but I remembered how proud they were to buy the buildings and set up the three shops.

Over a hundred years ago, when Spirit Town was a bustling market town, some enterprising newcomers had built this row of shops, near the primary school. Taking advantage of the fact that as the town grew, houses were being built on this side of town. Five corrugated iron peaked rooves adorned the wooden structure that was five semi-detached shop fronts. Each with its own front door and shop front window, letting customers peak inside to see what the store had to offer.

Over twenty years ago, I'd helped my parents with minor repairs inside and paint each building inside and out. Each shop was distinguished by a different colour exterior; blue, pink, yellow, green and orange. While the paint was a little faded the colours still made me smile on the inside.

As I drove up today, my stomach-ache grew worse, as if someone had punched me. I recognised the people standing out the front of the convenience store. Tanya managed the laundrette; she had a tribe of children who worked there for pocket money. In her mid-forties, my parents had seen a spark of independence and determination in her mother; the role passed to Tanya a few years ago. Her short colourful hair matched her tied dyed jumpsuit perfectly. Mary was one of the seamstresses. In her late fifties, Mary's hair was pulled back into a tight, bouncy ponytail. Her navy smock was sombre and serious next to the flamboyant colours of the jumpsuit. Mary's sisters helped out with repairs and alterations. Glen owned the convenience store. Once he retired from years driving trucks, he was happy for the quiet life, reading books and serving customers. He bought the store a few years ago, Around the same time that Jan bought the green grocers. She had managed it for my parents for years; she knew all the farmers and what they sold. Farmers appreciated a permanent market for their produce. Mike managed the wood shop. Fit and healthy for a seventy-year-old, a lifelong friend of Dad's having worked together for years, he still crafted amazing toys from cedar and cypress, showcasing them and other works of art from local wood crafters in the shop.

Clutching pieces of paper, the group were speaking animatedly, a couple of them waving their arms to make their point of view clearer.

I pulled my car into a space in front of the row of shops.

Most of the streets in our town were wide, not narrow like some of the streets in the bigger cities. Cars parked on the side of the road didn't impact traffic at all. With additional parking behind the buildings, I wasn't worried about customers not finding a parking spot.

"Good morning," I said, joining the group. A chorus of good morning from the five, all of whom I had known since I was small.

"Great timing," Tanya said, handing me her copy of the letter. "Each of us found this tucked under our door this morning." Her hand shook as she passed the letter to me to read. Glen paced across the pavement in front of the shops. Mary's agitation was evident, she twisted and crumpled the piece of paper in her hands. Mike was heavy set, a footballer of many years. He stood firmly, as if to shove away any attempt to take the shops. Jan stood tall and thin, elegant, and foreboding. If any of the shop keepers were gifted, she would be the one. Still, the group wouldn't be any match to bulldozers and a demolition crew.

I scanned the letter. It was on formal council letterhead. The letter told the shop operator they had until close of business tomorrow to shut their shop. Demolition would start on Thursday. It was signed by Max, as the mayor.

It's so easy to make a formal letter look official enough that people wouldn't question its legitimacy. As mayor, Max would find it easy to bluff and intimidate residents who trusted him, or with less business knowledge. He may not have realised that I owned three of the businesses.

"This letter is a hoax. It's not an official request to vacate," I told them. "Max is no longer the mayor. Ross Mac's the interim mayor until we can vote for a new one. Listen to the radio this morning, Ross is coming on to talk about this and other things. I'm running more information in the paper this week. If you get any other mail else like this, please let me know. No one is going to take away your businesses." As I spoke, a low, thick sticky fog started forming at the door of the grocers. It spread out left and right until it set a barrier across the entry to each shop.

"Jan!" Mike ruffled the top of his balding head. "We don't want to scare the customers. Don't you have a spell that's invisible, but still protects us from all this nonsense?"

I spent the next half an hour reassuring them that everything was okay. I brought some bananas and apples from Jan at the greengrocers, and some chocolate biscuits and an orange cake from Glen at the convenience store. I took a selection of each into the laundrette, the seamstress and the men's shed. Tanya, Mary, Glen, Mike and Jan were each grateful for the time and attention. I promised to get back to visit again later in the week. I hadn't meant to neglect my other businesses.

The next vision appeared as I was getting out of my car at work. The scene in front of me: cars and buses driving along a street, people walking briskly along the footpath—not talking to each other, preoccupied on their way to somewhere important. I saw a modern built shopping centre complex, with a multi storey hotel above it. I couldn't quite make out the name on the top. The development looked like a castle or a palace. It felt like a casino. Lots of clues there to unpack. As I ducked into the café to pre-order the sandwiches I had promised, someone brushed past me. I instantly felt a cold shiver run the length of my spine.

"Are you okay?" asked Evie.

"Yep, all good. Who was that?" I asked, pointing, so she would know I was referring to the man in the suit leaving the café. The word *dodgy* popped into my head. *Shonky,* he was not someone to be trusted. My intuition yelled *warning.* A grating sound, like fingers running down the blackboard.

"Not sure, some bigwig from the big city. He ordered coffee and sat over there on his laptop for a while. He wanted to know where the council chambers were. Now how can I help?"

I ordered our lunch and instead of walking to the office, I quickened my pace and headed towards the council chambers. Ross and another councillor were greeting the strange man in the suit as I entered the building. I mouthed *watch out* to Ross. He nodded acknowledgment of what I said as he took the man whose dark suit matched his aura. into his office. I couldn't shake the foreboding that followed me back to the office.

THE NEWSPAPER OFFICE looked like a pet creche. Lexi was sitting cross-legged on the floor, in amongst upturned boxes, a couple of old coffee tins and lots of wool and ribbon. Spark was chasing a ball of string that Lexi was wriggling along the floor. I wasn't sure who was having the most fun.

I handed her a bottle of pineapple juice and a raspberry muffin from the café. "Ooh my favourite!" She put the ball down and stood up. Spark stopped chasing the ball and bounded to me in a huge leap. "We've had a wonderful time."

"I can tell," I smiled. "Were there any messages?"

"No, but we do have an issue. I wanted to show you in person, rather than try and explain over the phone." Lexi led me out to the back to the storeroom. Spark was gently rubbing his head under my chin; the best feeling in the world.

I held my kitten a little more tightly as I immediately realised something was very wrong. The roller door to the storeroom had twisted and buckled. It looked like someone had pushed through with a shopping trolley full of heavy items. The palette of newspapers I would expect to see sitting in the corner of the covered verandah area wasn't there.

"Has Fred already picked up the papers for delivery?" I asked hopefully as that sinking feeling in the pit of my stomach returned.

"No."

As Lexi spoke, I felt my stomach lurch. I grabbed Spark a little more tightly, worried I would drop him. An image of Max, the person I saw talking to Ross and some other men in suits flashed into my head, standing outside that same building in the city. The name above their heads was *Castle Home*. The rest of the sign was obscured. Filing that image away, I listened to Lexi. "I rang the printers. They dropped the palette here as always. They thought it was odd that the delivery truck was already here. The driver assured them that he just wanted to get an early start as he had other deliveries to make. When Jake, our regular delivery driver, arrived to pick up the palette he rang me. That's when I saw the door was smashed in. All the festival brochure inserts are ruined. Someone has poured paint and oil all over them." She looked stricken. "I couldn't tell you over the phone. I've rung my builder mate Jock. He can remove the door and replace it later this afternoon. He's bringing some off-siders to clean up the mess inside and take all the rubbish to the tip. The printers are re-printing the inserts and today's edition of the paper. They can't deliver until after five tomorrow morning. Jake's lined up to deliver as soon as they arrive, and Jock's arranging a better security camera." She pointed to hole in the eaves of the verandah, where the camera should have been. "If you need me to, I can stay here tonight, to make sure nothing else happens."

"That means a lot, Lexi." Holding Spark out of the way I gave her a hug, before handing him to her. He knew she needed him, and he nuzzled her chin, purring loudly.

"I know it looked like I'd been on the floor with Spark for ages, but I only joined him after I organised everything as best I could." Lexi was close to tears. Her adrenalin had spurred her on to fix the situation. Now that she'd told me, she could let her defence down a little.

"I appreciate your determination, your tenacity and your loyalty. You organised it all, just as I'd have done. Do you need to take the rest of the day off? I appreciate your offer to stay overnight, that was very brave of you, but I'll ask Jon to have one of his officers keep watch."

"I'd rather keep working. I want to be here when Jock and his team arrive. I'd miss Spark if I went home, unless you're letting me take him with me." She grinned.

I smiled as I held out my arms for my familiar. "Why don't you take a break, have your muffin and your juice? Or maybe go for a walk, grab some more supplies. I was going out around two pm, but I am not sure if I will anymore."

Lexi nodded and passed Spark back to me. "I won't be long. I'll keep the juice and muffin as an afternoon snack." She quickly picked up Spark's bedding and toys and dropped them in my office. "Oh, and if Jock arrives before I get back, he looks rough, but he has a heart of gold. He used to play football, and he was on the boxing team for a while. If we need added security, he might be good as a deterrent."

"Thanks. I'll bear that in mind. I'll pop your muffin and juice in the kitchen. I want to make a cuppa and work out my next move." I wished I knew more about my powers, That spell Jan wove to protect the shops, if I could do that around the office, how cool would that be?

Seated at my laptop, I let Spark have the run of my office, keeping an eye on his whereabouts. I only had to type *Castle Home* into the google search bar to find it was a relatively new business chain. The selling feature being the apartments situated above the shopping complex which featured a castle themed pub. Starting in the capital cities in Australia, it was rapidly branching out into regional towns and now choosing smaller towns to showcase its magnificence, bringing tourism in to revitalise dying towns. Except that our town didn't need revitalising. It wasn't dying. I may have been biased, but I'd have thought there should be information for all residents to be part of the decision-making process.

I stared more closely at the photo of the men shaking hands out the front of the newest Castle Home. I recognised one of the men. He was the dodgy suit I had followed to the council chambers. One of the other men looked familiar but I couldn't quite place him.

Review websites weren't quite so positive.

Castle Home destroyed our town. Loss of jobs, people forced to leave town as locals weren't given jobs. Skilled workers bought in from the bigger cities.

Small businesses forced to close. Demolished literally and figuratively when the bigger corporation can offer items at a much lower cost.

Visitors travel to stay at the accommodation at Castle Home and shop at the shops at the bottom of the Castle Home building. The tourists would often not leave the complex for the entire length of their stay.

My switch flipped. I was mostly fair and quiet, considering all options before taking a stand on a topic. I would speak up if there was a reason to. I did sometimes suffer anxiety, although I hated the label and rarely referred to this, even to myself. My stomach issues, while mostly food related, were linked to my anxiety levels. So was my lack of sleep, and my coffee and chocolate addiction.

Spark came over from where he was watching me and jumped up on my lap.

I did wonder if I suffered obsessive compulsive disorder and maybe attention deficit as well. I knew it was trendy to have one of these afflictions, and so I didn't consider this lightly. If something annoyed me enough, or people weren't being treated unfairly, I would fight. I didn't mind speaking in public. I didn't get nervous in crowds or in unfamiliar situations. My zodiac sign was Leo, so I loved the limelight. I wasn't willing to let Max and his cronies win. I picked up my phone and sent a text to Lara.

Change of plan, please pick up the lunch I ordered from the café and come to the office. Bring Jon and Seamus too. Two pm as planned. Thanks.

My next text was to Ross.

I have more news. Please come to my office two pm.

I sent a similar one to Izzie. The only difference was that at the end of hers I added,

bring cake, please.

I took Spark with me to the meeting room. We sometimes called it the conference room, but it really wasn't that flash. The table sat ten people, twelve if we brought in more chairs. I laid the additional six chairs that stayed stacked in the corner around the table. It was perfect for spreading out our newspaper copy.

"Was our video session in here only last week?" I spoke softly to Spark. "It feels like ages ago." So much was happening. A major draw card of our little town was that it didn't have the drama and noise of the bigger cities. With Max gone now, hopefully things would calm down and get back to normal.

The clock on the wall told me it was only just after one. It felt much later.

I filled up a saucer with water for Spark and placed a small amount of food on a plate for him. Such a heartwarming sight, watching him daintily nibble his food.

The apple in the fruit bowl looked okay, although I couldn't remember when I bought it. I bit into an extra juicy pink lady apple. I filled a glass with tap water and skulled the whole lot. I refilled the glass and drained it as well. I would restock the kitchen with fruits and juices once things settled down.

"You probably should lock that door, if no one is in the office." Ross came around the side of the front counter. The look on his face told me he was half-joking, half-serious. "I received information this morning that the paper had some problems. Is everything okay? This morning was back-to-back meetings, I came over as soon as I could. I'm early, but if I'd stayed in my office there would've been some other drama to deal with."

"Come, have a seat. We can see the front door from here." Behind Lexi's counter there were two seats. Lexi often interviewed clients here, she said it was cosier than the larger room. Spark finished eating and ran over to meet Ross.

"Long story, for later," I said referring to Spark, who decided to chase the black shoelaces in Ross's shiny black shoes. "Did the well-dressed stranger tell you about the problems at the paper?"

"Yes, he did," Ross replied.

"And did he tell you about a marvellous opportunity to bring jobs and tourism to the town, a monstrosity called Castle Home?"

"I remember your awesome investigative skills. You should be a reporter," Ross quipped. "The well-dressed man from the city—his name is Brad. He and Wayne Smith, one of the councillors, were trying to convince me that it's the best and only logical next step for our council, and I should reinstate Max's demolition and construction order. I refused. They then made some veiled threat about problems in the town. Like the troubles you're having here. Inferring that incidents would continue unless I agreed with his proposal. I stood my ground."

"They stole today's edition of the paper and ruined the festival inserts. We have it under control. I'll not let Max and his cronies ruin our town." My stubbornness and determination had returned tenfold since Spark's arrival.

"That's the spirit," Seamus said, as he, Jon and Lara arrived, walking through the door seconds before Lexi and Izzie.

"What's happened?" Lara placed a plate piled high with little triangle sandwiches in the middle of the table. Seamus placed half a dozen bottles of juice next to the tray. Izzie added her stash of muffins and cakes to the table.

Ross and I joined the group at the table. Lexi ducked to the kitchen, returning with a stack of red paper serviettes. "Short version is that Max was working with a corporation in the city who want to build a monstrosity here, a large hotel and shopping complex. As well as being responsible for all the incidents over the last week, they're now pressuring businesses and council to approve their plans." I smiled at my assistant, who was passing the plate of sandwiches around. "Lexi has been amazing. She's single-handedly organised the re-printing of the latest edition of the paper, which was stolen early this morning, as well as new festival magazines which were destroyed."

Ross ran his hand through his greying hair. His short hair still had the tinge of red I remembered from years ago. We were the same height, making him one of the shortest males in our class through high school. We used to joke that we were waiting for his growth spurt. It never happened. "Max and at least one other councillor have been working with a group in the city to create a gaudy tourist attraction in our town. In the extraordinary council meeting today, I managed to revoke Max's motion to demolish the Wynyard Street row of shops. I garnered support from five of the seven other council members. Wayne Smith and Trevor Howard support Max's motion. Brad Walden is the dodgy city suit."

"I'm interviewing Ross at four this afternoon," Izzie spoke up. Although we were close in age, her energy levels were ten times higher than mine. She was well rounded, athletically built and had the most jovial mischievous face of anyone I had ever met. "We need to let the town know what's happening. We can report the facts; like the mayor had passed the motion to demolish the shops under the radar, no consultation and the shopkeepers only receiving the letters to vacant this morning, we don't know where the mayor is, and he was behind all the trouble in the town recently. All these can be corroborated as factual."

"Let's finish off the sandwiches and the cakes, to fortify ourselves for the afternoon." I suggested. Silence fell as we all munched on something from the table. There was a lot to think about. We watched as Spark crept and pounced at everyone's feet. Like a little feather duster, tickling and spreading love everywhere he went.

It was Jon who broke the silence. "Knowing Max was involved with the Castle Town corporation is helpful. Myra may be able to trace money and some contractual stuff to them. We've an officer watching their offices. Myra's talking to our legal eagles, to make sure we have a tight case, before we attempt to arrest anyone." He rubbed his temple. I could feel the beginnings of his migraine thumping in behind my temples. One of the downfalls of being an empath. If I didn't spend a few minutes in the morning, putting on my invisible purple coat of protection, I'd often feel the illnesses and emotions of those around me. I felt his exhaustion.

"The good news—no one in town liked Max. Most of the customers I spoke to this morning distrust all the councillors, which is normal. People are good at complaining about people in authority but will refuse to step up and do something about it. We can expect more dissatisfaction once people hear the radio interview." Seamus's dark brown hair bounced around as he spoke. When he spoke, his whole body quivered the energy and passion he was feeling. I wondered if everyone else noticed this, or if it was just me.

"Izzie, is it possible for me to follow Ross, if you have enough airtime? I want to explain why the paper will be a day late. I think that's important for the locals to know." I was pretty sure Izzie would back me on this, but I thought it polite to ask.

"Of course!" Izzie said between mouthfuls of muffin.

Lara had been unusually quiet during lunch. Just before I asked why, she spoke, "My customers were angry about Max. Most of them suggested the same solution."

"And what was the solution?" I asked, interested in what people were thinking. There had been a lot going on in the town over the last week. People must be exhausted, frustrated, and worried. It was unsettling for everyone. Lara's clients were interested in health and wellness and making the best decisions, rather than getting drawn into drama.

"Their suggestion was that you stand for Mayor," she replied.

"Who? Me?" I couldn't believe what I heard.

"Yes. You spoke in public several times over the last week. Each time you calmed the situation. Diffused the anxiety. They trust you. I'm just passing on what I've been hearing." Lara shrugged her shoulders.

"I've heard similar," Seamus agreed. "Across the gifted community too. Mostly they like to live under the radar. Mr Moore confided to me that even Mrs Wiley and Mrs Marigold, welcome the thought of you as mayor." He paused for a few seconds. "I think it's because you live in both worlds now. It took you a while though."

"You've lived in both successfully for your whole life Seamus. You would be better at being mayor than me," I responded, humbled by the suggestion.

"Nah, I don't do public speaking, I am not an obsessive compulsive super-organised powerhouse of energy, and I don't delegate well," Seamus said. "I did think about it, for a whole minute, before I decided to defer to you. Beth for mayor." He smiled.

"Let's just deal with one challenge at a time." I wanted to get us back on track. I felt uncomfortable at the thought of being mayor, though Seamus did have a point about my bossy characteristics. "We've a town and a festival to save. Ross, you're okay to stay as interim mayor, aren't you?" I sensed a sense that he was regretting his choice to step in, even for the short term.

"Not really. I was keen to serve, but not as leader. This morning it felt like half a dozen knives were being aimed at my back. I must think of Belinda. We're trying for a baby and the stress of me as mayor, well, I don't want her to have to endure that. I'm going to suggest we hold an out of session, early election as soon as possible. Sorry Beth."

"Don't apologise Ross. Family and health come first. We'll support you as best we can." I looked around the room. Everyone nodded their support.

Izzie stood up, looking regretfully at the pile of muffins. "As much as I'd like to stay and chat, and eat, I'd better get ready for the interviews this afternoon. Thanks for lunch. I'll see you both soon." She carried Spark with her as far as the door. I followed her out. As she handed him back to me, she whispered, "You would make a good mayor. Honest, fair, impartial." Before I could respond, she was gone.

"We need a plan," Seamus was saying when I returned to the room. "You do have to call the early election; we get it mate." Ross nodded gloomily. "Beth, no pressure, but can you seriously think about whether you will put your hand up to be mayor?" I nodded, watching the others around the table.

Lexi was clearing the table of the leftover food, taking everything to the kitchen. Lara, who had taken Spark when I returned, tucked him into his carrier and was patting him. He was purring as his eyes were closing. Jon was making notes in his notepad.

"Jon, do you need anything from any of us?" I sensed his stress. Dealing with a group of teenage vandals could be challenging enough. Corporate crime that included elected officials and rich businessmen was something else entirely.

"This is a little out of my league," he admitted. "I'm going to meet my superiors this afternoon. I just hope none of them are working with Castle Home. With the financial implications, this all belongs in the fraud squad. Although we never needed the extra reinforcements, I think we need to keep the extra team here. It sounds like the suits are still sending people out to destroy papers, break in *et cetera*. From what you said, Ross, we are looking at one other corrupt councillor, maybe more."

"Yes." I gave Ross a hug as he got to his feet. He looked like he needed one.

"Don't think you're letting anyone down. Family comes first. I'll see you at the station in a little while," I told him. I walked Ross to the door. Jon followed behind.

"Can I walk with you and take notes?" he asked. Ross nodded. Jon turned back to me. "I'll update you later. I'll send Fred to check in on the office more frequently. We will increase the police presence overall. Sending a clear message."

"Thanks." Our conversation was cut short as Jock turned up with his two offsiders. I let them into the office, watching Jon and Ross walk to Ross's car. He loved his old Holden. He didn't drive it much, but it was a classic. I remembered it as his father's car—dropping us off to school some mornings, driving us to tennis practise. I was glad he had kept the vehicle. His dad would be very proud of the man Ross had become.

Lexi took Jock and the others straight out to the storage area. I returned to Seamus and Lara. "We waited to see if there is anything we can do for you," Lara said.

"Thanks guys, but honestly, I can't think of anything. Let me get the radio interview over with and catch my breath. I'll think about what we discussed. Me as mayor though? I don't think so." An image of me as mayor flashed before my eyes. I shook my head, to clear the image.

"We'll catch up later then." Seamus and Lara each gave me a quick hug.

I turned around as I heard someone behind me.

"I have everything under control here. I'll watch Spark while you do your interview."

"Thanks, Lexi. When I come back, we're going to lock up early, and go home, to think about anything but the events of the day. We'll be back bright and early tomorrow to focus on the new day. Is that a deal?"

"Yes, it is." Lexi smiled.

Chapter 17

I wasn't sure how I was feeling. Apart from exhausted, partly due to the active dreams, and the range of interactions throughout the day. The evenings temperature had dropped, as it did in the late afternoon during autumn. Any time after three was probably a good time to be indoors.

Instead, here I was, standing on our front verandah, with the big old wooden floorboards. The type of boards that look like they would outlast a flood. Not like the flimsy wood that pass as flooring today. The metre high wooden fence around the front and sides, a white picket fence, complete with a gate that allowed entry onto and out of the space. The gate was latched open most days, making it easier to come and go. The white wicker table and chairs were replicas of the old style popular in the seventies. The duck egg blue and white floral cushions on the chair blended well with the grey paint on the walls. This was one of my favourite places to hang out and watch the world pass by.

I loved sitting here as much as sitting in the library room full of books or wandering through the back garden with all the aromas and colours. Last year I gave the fence palings a fresh coat of paint. I added café blinds and an assortment of potted plants.

Spark was currently exploring these plants. He didn't damage any of the leaves as he climbed in amongst the bright blue ceramic pots filled with exotic looking plants with glossy leaves. Plants that I'd forgotten the names of. The tags that once told me had long since disappeared. It felt good to sit out in the fresh late afternoon air. The sun was setting behind the row of houses across the road. The chill in the air gave me goosebumps, but I didn't want to move to grab my cardigan which I'd left draped on a chair in the kitchen. The history of our family was infused and entwined, part of the furnishings and the very structure of my home. It was calming, sitting here, with whisperings of times past tickling my spirit. The tingling throughout my body, as my powers awakened, I had no name for it. Spirit was as close as I could find, to describe the sensation.

In front of me was my laptop and a large glass of water. I regretted deciding I needed water instead of a cup of tea or coffee. In hindsight I could have brought both water and a hot drink outside. My intuition told me not to move. I thought back over the events of the afternoon at the radio station.

Ross's chat with Izzie caused quite a stir. The phones ran hot with listeners dialling in to express their anger, outrage, and concern at the allegations against Max and the council in general. Most callers supported Ross. They said they all knew Max was not trustworthy. Izzie made it clear the information about Max and what he'd done were facts, with evidence to back every single accusation. By the time I entered the soundproof studio, Ross was pale. His normally tanned complexion drained, looking like clammy spoiled milk.

"I'm not cut out for this," he muttered at the end of his radio interview. A song from the eighties played for the viewers.

"You did beautifully!" Izzie soothed. "Everyone called to support what you're doing. Their anger is at Max, not you."

"I know, but the emotions and the passion." Ross shuddered. "Beth, I'm not just saying this because I don't want this role anymore. I've seen you talk to a crowd. Their emotions don't get to you like it does to me."

"I'll let you in on a secret," I told Ross. "It affects me just as much. I've just taught myself how to handle it. I can teach you too if you like."

"Sounds like something I should know how to do," he agreed. "Another time. Now I'm going home to have dinner with my amazing, supportive wife."

As Izzie walked with Ross to the door, I sat and looked around the studio, a soundproof booth approximately three metres square with lots of electrical technical equipment around the walls. Izzie's desk was covered with pieces of paper and a computer. Izzie had a system. I was pretty sure it was her superpower. Intuitively picking the stories and the interviews that mattered. Growing the audience and promoting the village and all it's businesses. She had a knack for organised chaos, remembering information without needing to make notes. Acing exams through high school and university, quietly and without big noting her ability.

"Okay, so that went well, despite what Ross thought. He became overwhelmed at the number of people who called in. He is competent, great at his job. But not a leader. I'll just put another song on." She pressed a few buttons on a machine in front of her. "Now are you ready? We'll start with the theft of the papers. You take the lead. I'll jump in with questions as it flows."

THE FIRST CALLER AFTER my interview asked if I was going to run for mayor. So did the second. The third told me it was all a bunch of lies and that Max should be mayor, that the town needed his vision and business acumen. Thankfully after caller number three it was time for the news.

ON MY LAPTOP, I BEGAN a pros and cons list. Why I should be mayor. The benefits and pitfalls to me and to the town. I couldn't shake the vision in my head of me as mayor. Breaking ground at a community garden project. The vision was clear. As was the feeling of accomplishment that came with it.

From my position I saw Agnes walking along the street. She made walking up the hill that led to my house look effortless, unlike the uncomfortable slope that I was faced with, whether I was approaching or leaving home. Agnes strolled like she was wandering through the park. As she made her way to my front gate, I stood and walked down the couple of steps to greet her. Spark followed at my heels, not interested in escaping. The best pet ever.

"Good afternoon," Agnes greeted me.

"Good afternoon, Agnes. Can I get you a cup of tea, or a glass of water?"

"No thank you. I'd like to sit a while with you, if you have time."

"Certainly." I led Agnes over to the table and positioned one of the chairs for her. Spark jumped up on her lap as soon as she did. She picked him up, kissed his forehead and placed him on my lap. Spark hopped up onto my right arm and snuggled into my neck.

"I see you're bonding well. You're finding your visions are clearer." It was a statement, not a question.

I nodded.

"I wanted to ask you something, on behalf of our community. Some of us heard you on the radio this afternoon." My chest tightened at her words. Was she unhappy with my chat with Izzie?

"You have to learn to trust yourself more child." Agnes softened her voice. "Not everything is a criticism. We heard you on the radio and we'd like to ask you to seriously consider running for mayor."

I was dumbfounded. That was the last thing I expected to hear from Agnes.

"You have the gifts of compassion, passion, and strength. You're loyal and fight for what you believe in. They're all good qualities. Together with your special abilities, which will grow and sharpen the more time you spend with Spark. Our town needs a person with those qualities." Agnes leant across the table, touching my left hand. I felt a tingle of energy starting at the tips of my fingers, rush up my left arm, around my shoulders and back down my right arm.

"Listen to your heart. Pay attention to your inner voice. Feel the energy of those around you. Give yourself one term as mayor, see how the town changes." Agnes could see my fear and self-doubt. I wondered if it was possible. "You can do it. Our gathering has just approved endorsing you as our candidate. We've never endorsed anyone before. It wasn't my idea. Some of the others heard you speak in the crowd and on the radio. They asked me to talk to you." Having said her piece, Agnes sat back. I could feel her eyes assessing my reaction.

I sat back in my chair. The cool evening wind was tickling my ankles, and buffeting my shoulders, gently. I felt propelled forward. The message to move into the flow of the energy. I smiled as I saw myself in the mayor's office. There was a lightness of energy, excitement and moving forward.

"You can feel it too," Agnes stated. I nodded.

"There's so much possibility. If you trust yourself." With another stare that pierced my spirit, joining with it, strengthening it, she rose to her feet. "I must go. Thank you for your time and consideration. We will work together soon." She was gone before I could say goodbye.

An image of the swinging door at the café appeared just as Jon climbed up the steps. Agnes was right about the heightening of my senses. "I saw you talking to Agnes as I drove past. Have you got a minute to chat?"

"Absolutely. You'll distract me from the other things wading through my mind." I was relieved for the distraction. After my discussion with Agnes there was no longer any doubt about what I had to do.

"Who wants ice cream?" Seamus called out as he and Lara hopped out of her car before Jon had a chance to share his news. "We met at the café and Lara said you would probably feel like ice cream, so here we are."

"Perfect timing, guys. Jon, there are a couple of extra seats around the corner, I'll go and get some bowls and spoons." When I returned, they were gathered around the table. Someone had closed my laptop. Spark was on Lara's lap, trying to get into the tub of ice cream.

Jon launched straight into what was on his mind. "The fraud squad can prove Max wasn't acting in the best interest of the town. I think the corporation deliberately made it easy for us to track the money, so he'd end up in prison. Max was their scapegoat. Expendable. Greedy. Looking to benefit himself and not our town. The head of the Castle Home will pay a penalty but will avoid gaol time. They won't be building Castle Home in our town. We identified the other two council members who deliberately misrepresented the town for financial gain."

"If Ross hadn't already called an out of session meeting and election, we would've had to force one. We've asked for the resignation of Wayne and Trevor. That leaves Ross and three councillors. Ross will ask for nominees tomorrow. People will have five days to nominate, and the election can be held five days after that." Everyone investigated their laps, like me, thinking through the implications of Jon's words.

Time for change.

"I've decided to nominate as mayor. Agnes came by this afternoon to advise me the supernatural members of our community will support my nomination." I allowed myself a smile as Spark kneaded my lap. Purring as loudly as ever. No one spoke for what felt like ages. It was Seamus who broke the silence.

"You have my support. I was thinking of nominating for a position on council. It feels like the perfect time to give back to the community." I had never used the word nervous when describing Seamus, yet right now, his tone of voice gave it away. I repressed the urge to hug him. The last thing Seamus wanted was a fuss. His many qualities made him the perfect representative.

"You both have my support," Lara whispered. "My strength is in the background. I can make banners, signs, advertising, that sort of thing. Oh gosh I'm sure you will both get voted in."

I was about to thank Lara when I remembered I had called a festival committee meeting. I looked at my watch, in ten minutes.

Lara saw me glancing at my timepiece, an old-fashioned silver-plated watch with a stretchy metal band, given to me by my parents at my graduation. Not one of those new smart watches that counted my steps, although all things considered that would be handy sometimes. "I postponed the festival meeting until nine tomorrow morning. The members of the committee heard you on the radio and were happy to convene tomorrow. I even got hold of Juliet. She ran, left town, when Max left. She didn't do anything wrong, except she knew what he was up to, and she didn't try to stop him." Lara turned to Jon, "Juliet will ring you tomorrow. She had to tell her parents first, she isn't sure what will happen once she tells you what she knows."

"Thanks Lara, I totally forgot about the committee with all the talk about becoming mayor. Good work talking to Juliet as well."

Jon took his notepad out of his pocket and wrote a few words. "Fred found the thieves who stole the papers and destroyed the magazines. They were from out of town and were happy to dob in their contact at the consortium behind Castle Home.

"It seems like a celebration is in order. Luckily our ice cream hasn't melted. Who wants choc peppermint fudge?" Seamus was acting jovial, but I could feel his anxiety. Smiling reassuringly, I caught his eye.

SPARK AND I WOKE UP at five the next morning. Once Spark was set up at the office with Lexi for company, I walked around the corner to the council office. As it didn't open until eight thirty, I debated going to grab myself a coffee. Seamus solved my dilemma, arriving a few minutes later with coffee and a berry muffin each.

"That's one thing I can tick off my ever-growing list of things to worry about," I said, showing Seamus the text from Lexi.

Papers and inserts safely arrived and delivered.

I knew he was still nervous about his decision. He was quiet. Not his jovial self at all.

"I do appreciate you nominating with me," I said quietly.

"It's only half for you," he admitted, just as quietly. "I want to do this for me. I meant what I said. This town has been good to me, and others like me—like us. I want to spend some time giving back."

Ross opened the door right on eight thirty. "Boy, am I glad to see you both. I couldn't sleep all night worrying that no one would want to nominate. It's not exactly a glamourous or exciting gig."

Like all forms, the paperwork took longer than expected.

Seamus and I arrived at the committee meeting as Lexi was offering around cups of tea or coffee. Considering the issues at council, we had agreed to meet in our conference room. I glanced around the table. Harry Field, Doc Syder, Mrs Olde, Glenda, and Lara; full attendance. "Juliet sends her apologies. She is dealing with some family issues and is unavailable. I'd like to propose that Lara steps into Juliet's role for the remainder of this year's festivities." Lara had agreed via text when I'd proposed this to her only ten minutes previously. No one disagreed, so I sat down and let Lara chair the meeting.

THE NEXT FEW DAYS WERE quiet. The news that the Castle Home development might be going ahead in either of the neighbouring towns, Apple Tree or Flowerville didn't come as a surprise. Apple Tree was bigger than Spirit Town; farms consisting of rows of orchards growing oranges, pears, peaches, cherries, and apples kept business booming and a steady stream of visitors and seasonal fruit pickers. Flowerville was more of a foodie town, though it's annual festival celebrated sunflowers, roses and other edible flowers. The rich soil was certainly a bonus for anyone brave enough to choose farming as a vocation.

"I wish them all the best, trying to get that monstrosity past any of our local communities." Lexi's fingers tapped quickly on the keyboard of her laptop. "The gifted and the not so gifted, we all want local businesses to succeed. No one's keen for the money to leave the village and end up in the hands of the big city corporations. Izzie and I have this idea to interview some of the local farmers, and maybe a couple of local business owners. To talk about the problems we had here, and maybe the people in the neighbouring towns will be able to stop the development going ahead. None of the locals want to see a casino built on our doorstep. "Once the festival celebrations are over, I'd like to spotlight some of our local farmers, describing a day in the life of living on the farm."

"I've every confidence in your ideas. I love that you and Izzie are going to work closely on this. The paper is in safe hands with you in charge, if I was to be successful with my nomination." Lexi shuffled her feet under the table, her fingers typing even more furiously on the keyboard at my praise.

"We have at least ten additional volunteers," Lara said excitedly. It was the Wednesday before the festival; we were meeting for an early dinner at Evie's café. The café was even busier than usual. Lots of visitors had arrived in town for the weekend's festivities. Word had spread around neighbouring towns that there had been unusual incidents. People were coming to check out what all the fuss was about. "We've had so many enquiries about the festival, offers of volunteers, people wanting to make a weekend of it. Everyone's being super helpful."

"Pizzas and curly fries, with mochas and ginger beer," Evie declared, placing the dishes in front of us. I looked over at Seamus, whose turn it had been to order dinner. He merely shrugged and smiled, before picking up a piece of pizza.

"Max and the other councillors are facing court next week," Jon confirmed. "Thank goodness it's all over with. The other officers can go back to the city after Saturday."

THE WARMTH OF THE SUN of the back of my neck always relaxed me. The autumn winds were kind to us, bothering some other town on this glorious morning.

The Spirit Festival Parade. Witches, wizards, ghosts, ghouls, goblins, and skeletons. As many in the crowd as on the floats. The school float was huge, thanks to the local trucking company loaning them two vehicles. A couple of the smaller children looked terrified of the haunted house on wheels as it drove slowly past where we were all gathered to watch the parade. The black trailer cover of the transport company was the perfect backdrop for ghoulish decorations. Each community group had made an effort, each school, and organisation had entered something in the parade. Local sports teams too, although their focus seemed to be the entries for the land boat race. Of the ten boat race entries, only one made it all the way over the finish line. They beat the men's and women's basketball team, three football teams, the cricket team, the swimmers and the lawn bowls. It was great to see the Neilson children with big smiles on their faces as they received their trophy.

I was so busy volunteering, as chaperon to show visitors around our town, that I gave in when Seamus tempted me with a dagwood dog and curly potatoes at three in the afternoon. I declined the offer of more carnival food, opting instead to walk home and have a much-needed rest.

"You passed your test with flying colours!" I scooped Spark up, out of the makeshift play pen Lexi and I had erected early this morning. We had taken it in turns to check on Spark throughout the day. "I suspect Lexi spent more time here than at the festival." I crooned, snuggling Spark, breathing in that gorgeous kitten smell that was almost intoxicating. "I'm exhausted. It was a huge day, successful, every seemed to be having fun." Spark purred, our energies vibrating together as one.

My mug of tea in one hand, my laptop in the other, Spark followed as I led the way to bed.

"YOU DID A FANTASTIC job as master of ceremonies," I said to Ross as we walked along Tumble Street early on Sunday morning.

"It was easy, knowing it was a one off and that the new mayor will have that and all the other public speaking jobs from nine tomorrow morning. I will never be able to thank you enough for nominating and accepting the role. I'm glad you were the only person to nominate, it makes it much easier." He grinned. "Thanks for agreeing to the handover today. Belinda and I are spending some time away, a holiday at our favourite cabin at the beach. We're leaving early tomorrow morning."

"You deserve the break after the last few weeks. I'm sure you'll have a lovely time." I sighed. The sort of sigh that acknowledged excitement and anticipation. "I think I'm looking forward to this new chapter in my life. It feels right." The air around us was crisp and cool. My senses were heightened, the colours vibrant, the smells and sounds, as if it was all on stereo. I was excited and nervous, not just at the thought of my new role, but because my extraordinary powers were awakening.

"What about Spark?" Ross asked. "I don't see you leaving him home all day."

"Between Lexi and I, we have Spark covered. Lara is willing to kitten sit too if needed." I wasn't sure what I thought of leaving Spark for such a long period of time each day. I was willing to give it a go, to believe in the bigger picture, and that somehow it would work out.

Seamus met us at the park bench just outside Ross's office. The street was lined with poplars, showing off their vibrant golden autumn shades. "Are you sure you want me here too?"

"Of course. You'll remember the parts I forget." I smiled. That's how it had always worked between us. As the poplars' autumn leaves fell around us, I looked forward to the next chapter.

The End

Sarah Lewin

If you want to know more about me or my books, here are some details. Alternatively, please make contact via any of the social media listed below:

Email: sarahlewin@sarahlewin.com.au

You Tube: https://youtube.com/@sarahlewinangelwisdom539

Blog: https://sarahlewin.com

Facebook: https://www.facebook.com/SarahLewinAuthorWitchyMysteryBooks

Instagram: https://www.instagram.com/sarahlewin_author/

Amazon: https://amazon.com/author/sarahlewin

Goodreads: https://www.goodreads.com/author/show/43342156.Sarah_Lewin

Book Bub: https://www.bookbub.com/authors/sarah-lewin

My Witchy Mystery Books:

<u>Witch Wisdom Series:</u>

#1 – Crone Wisdom

#2 – Ancient Wisdom

<u>Spirit Town Cosy Mysteries:</u>

#1 – Autumn Leaves are Falling

Book #2 – Available Soon

<u>I also have a range of children's books available.</u>